Disclaimer: This is a work of fiction, any portrayal for real persons or places is merely coincidental.

© 2023 by Armanis Ar-feinial

ISBN: Paperback: 979-8-9861041-7-1

ISBN: Ebook: 979-8-9861041-6-4

Table of Contents:

Author's Note:
Ohayou!
Thank you for looking inside this book. There is one thing you absolutely need to know before reading. The story of Lira is told in a very unorthodox manner, and I fully expect most of you to give up and put it on a DNF list. Once you get through the first page, you'll know how much you can stomach in relation to how it's being told. If at the end, you finish it, please leave a review, I do so love your comments, good or bad. Yes, you can read this book by itself.

Lira
Land of Dreams

Part One

I kindly suggest you go to Hell. First off, you come here, unwelcomed into my Mother's Sacred Tree. Yes, yes, I understand the likes of you think it's cursed, but why would you even come inside a cursed tree? Educated, my ass!

Just what, exactly? Come to tear out the heart strings then?

And you come to a bard instead of your damned necromancer down below? Morgresm has a death kink. Much more useful to him dead than alive, I should think. You want to know what you're feeling and why you're feeling this way? Am I correct in this assessment?

I understand then, frail little boy. Let me tell you a story, as Mother has an interest in adopting you. That's why you were compelled here. But first, remember the beggar your sister, Sar, mutilated a few short weeks ago? Oh, don't look at me like that; Mother made it known to me. Sar cut his fingers and nose off and sent him off by himself with soiled food in the damned acid rain.

Mother is she who birthed this world the way it ought to be, before we destroyed it. And the world you see is the tragic result of such a calamity. How did we destroy it? Simple. We didn't listen to one another. Some stubborn mule concluded that human beings cannot understand one another, and they never will. He was right. They never will. And the gates of Hell opened, and Nezka came up, helped rebuild the world into the dark repressive regime your family now rule over. That was, of course, until the Nezka sought race superiority and mercilessly raped and pillaged like the Vikings in ancient times.

Vikings? Oh, you don't need to concern yourself with them. They're long gone. Now, let's bring our focus back, you came here to get help from me because you don't understand why you're feeling the way you do. It was about that beggar, but it's more than that. There is a word that has since been lost in your vocabulary, you piece of shit. All you royal broods are pieces of shits!

Your hearts are rotten. They're all fucking rotten!

Black, pruned, wrinkling with old aged. Soiled, and good for nothing but to be dust in the wind, and return to dust from whence you came, Alkel. And yet, Mother still wants you for some reason. That, ultimately, is the reason you're here. Another replacement. How will you fare? Hanged from the room that you sleep in? Or maybe Sar will slit your throat just as you sit upon the throne after killing your father? Will she poison you? Or make you a cuckold first? So many ways to go, and you're running out of time.

Soft words go a long way, which was an idiom from my time, before the walls rose from nothing. Well, Mother created them to protect you all from the monsters outside them. Well, welcome to a dystopia. It's Hell inside, and if you can imagine, it's worse outside. No water, no hope, nothing but dead, and unnamed creatures that will eat you in a gulp, giants with toes as large as your castle. Discomforting, isn't it?

Now, Alkel, I must admit, while you and your family didn't create this Hell, you perpetuate it, by simply doing nothing and leaving your people to their own devices to eat one another, kill one another for scraps. Oh? You didn't know this? How ignorant could you possibly be!

Sit tight, you're gonna be here for a while. Don't bother looking for a way out. As you can see, the door is sealed, with no cracks to pry it open. Mother wants you here, and she's bewitched you. You will hear me tell a story. The story of a little girl who's not seen eleven revolutions around the sun.

The sun? You don't know what the sun is? What the hell is wrong with you! It's a giant yellow orb in the sky that keeps us from skirting off into distant worlds! Of course, you don't know this. Those blasted black clouds keep any and all manner of light from the veil of the world shining its rays upon us. You won't know what a star is either. Silly me. Fuck!

She's eleven years old. Alkel, can you get that through your thick brain? Good. Now to provide some setting. But I must warn you first, get that pail, you're gonna throw up. I must provide some details about the setting because you've never seen what your subjects live in, have you?

You enjoy a good night's sleep, right? You have a nice hay bed, covered in blankets, and some pillows, filled with whatever you deranged lunatics stuff in them, to provide support to your neck when you sleep. Your bed is appropriately lifted to permit you enough ease to move to the floor. You get to choose how high it is. Oh, how could I forget this, you prissy hussies even have clothes to sleep in! Now, given this, what do you think your subjects sleep in?

Your younger sister, Rach, she's about the same age as Lira, younger even. She's beautiful, with a full head of hair, neatly tied up when the occasion calls for it. A lovely, beautiful gown, and she's just right. Her body is slender, yet her skin doesn't uncomfortably cling to her bones. A smile on her face creeps upon her lips sometimes. Only sometimes, I wonder why? What does Mother have planned for her, I wonder?

Don't interrupt me, Alkel! Like I said, you can't leave.

If it was so easy, I'd be dead already, now shut up and listen while I go in outrageous detail. Create a mental image in your head, okay? Do you have an image of Rach in your head? Good. Now imagine her underneath all those covers, resting peacefully on that bed of hay. You have that?

Oh, and those pillows adequately stuffed in Mother only knows what. Probably dung pile, you degenerate perverts. Now, where was I? Oh yes. Now, I want you to remove the blanket, and you should picture her sleeping, curled up like a rock, holding to those clothes of hers tightly. Still with me? Now, take those pillows away, and now she's just resting on the hay. Not comfortable at all is it?

But wait, there's more. Or should I say less? That hair of hers, full it is now, but I want you to imagine you can see the individual strands of hair are like wires on her head, and you can see near perfectly the curvature of her skull. Not too pleasant, is it? Less? Oh yes, less even. Take off her clothes. Take them all off.

Excuse me.

The skin, I want you to take a good look at it. Her limbs are withered, not like the arms and legs of the sister you know. Not strong at all. Perhaps sturdy enough to get her from one part of town to the other, but for her to get caught in a fit of acid rain, one would think her skin would just fall off like melting meat. Move your eyes up from her legs to the abdomen, her belly, if you will. It looks like a bowl, pushing in and out with each breath, and if you look even further to just below her chest, her ribs are well defined.

Need I remind you that you perpetuate this tragedy by not doing anything. You want change? You're the only one with influence able to do anything about it. Now, grow a pair, and stop bein' a diminutive bitch.

And now, if that wasn't cruel enough, why don't you add a few inches from the bed to the floor, high enough that someone as small as Rach might break a few bones if she fell. Might I bring attention to the bed now? It isn't hay. Picture a giant slab of stone cracked in a number of places.

Let's talk about the bedroom now, Alkel. Let's talk about it. It's black. Why? Because there are no candles for her to light, and the torch-light from outside is far enough away that it doesn't even touch the front door. Lira resides and sleeps on the second floor of this building, an iron box with rust and lead and other foul germs in the air: rot.

Now, before you interrupt me, allow me to take you back to the day your sister cut the girl's father into pieces. How's that sound? Do you like the idea of revisiting an event you could have prevented? Or too afraid, are you? Yes, I know all about it. Your father hates you. Your mother hates you, and Sar would sooner kill you out of her own personal enjoyment, of course. Regrettably, her life will be too short. Or rather, yours too long. You know as well as I do your life is near its end; it will be decided should things not change shortly after your father's death, which I might add is right around the corner.

Now, get your brain back in this shithole. Do you remember the room? What it looks like with Rach in it? You have that picture? I want you picturing Rach for this, though her name in this tale is Lira, and I will call her such. Nod if you have it pictured. She's naked, remember?

Yawning and stretching, rolling over the side, Lira sweeps her legs off the side of the stone slab and hops off, landing casually on the ground, nearly slipping. She manages to walk blindly to the other side of the room. There's a small metal canister—

Why is everything metal? I don't know. I wasn't there, but Nezka and humans fashioned structures out of sheet metal and left them there to age, rust, and rot. These structures had several things resembling what I used to call trash cans in them. A word that existed at the time. You call them rubbish barrels.

She looked into the canister, dark and black as it was, and reached in, one hand straining against the near sharpened edge, slicing into her palm. She hissed, pulling out her shirt and trousers. She put them on. From the pants, she felt a draft, and her tunic was all threads. You could see right through it.

Why keep those clothes in a canister that would cut her? Well, Alkel, clothes are really hard to come by, especially for the likes of her. It was not unusual for someone to rummage throughout the houses for valuables they might steal. The sharp canister would serve its purpose and reduce the likelihood that someone would steal them from poor Lira.

And now, she stepped out of the corner, into the darkened hallway. Her hand touched the cold iron wall, and her feet inched forward until she felt nothing below it, cautiously stepping down each individual stair. One by one, in the dark, no windows, no moisture in the air even. A miserable place, wouldn't you agree?

Getting down to the bottom of the stairs, she grabbed hold of the corner, leading her into her hovel's kitchen. She climbed through, carefully feeling her way through the room. She passed over debris of so many kinds. Bags, chairs, stools, boxes, miscellaneous metal bars (I wonder why he even had those there). She made it safely to the counter, and opened a drawer, heavy it was, pulled out some tinder, and lit up the room.

Seeing the mangled mess of it, she pulled the stool closer to the kitchen counter, climbed the support of the chair like a ladder, and drew the candle closer, lighting it. You see, Alkel, the destitute don't have the luxury of living in places they can fix up. Everything was like it was, before she and her father came here. The chairs are larger than the ones you'd find in your castle, humans used to be taller, believe it or not. Her belly was hungry, and her lips chaffed with thirst. She heard a groan coming from the other end of the room.

Her head swiveled and she saw her father. Do I even need to remind you what he looked like before your sister mutilated him? You know what he looks like. You remember the despair, the desperation, and the utter helplessness in his eyes. The blank stare. The frail bones, the limbs with the skin pulled back to the cold, hard floor. Empty, just like his daughter, Lira, a bowl for a tummy with nothing inside and ribs that you can crack with a simple flick of a finger.

Can you picture it, Alkel? Can you? Because I've a pretty vivid image in my head.

This is what Lira sees, every morning. She felt something in her, the desire to help someone in need, regardless of the need she herself had. She stepped wearily outside, the torch lighting the pathway, the cobblestones leading to the road. Those green orbs? You see them as they signify the time of day that people should be up. You see, it was so early that even those weren't lit up yet.

She crouched down, her hand wiping the dirt, the soil in between each stone, and grabbed a fistful. Bringing it to her face, she herself ate it, dry and sore to her lips, drying out her tongue.

Alkel, don't fucking look at me like that! They have no food; what do you expect they eat? If only to stave off the hunger pangs.

Anyway, the dirt stuck in her gums, and she licked the stones out, her own blood coating them. She grabbed another handful. Why would she do that? Because her father had yet to eat, and so she brought some of those precious minerals to him.

So, she did. Knelt beside him, hands over her father's expressionless face. Her hand shook over him, tears rolled down that malnourished face. No movement at all. None from her dear papa.

You think you have it rough? At least your abusive father acknowledges you when you're in the damned room!

"Papa," she said, "Ye need to eat. Ye'll die if ye don't."

And he didn't muster a movement. None at all. No twitches in his feet, legs, even his lips didn't budge.

"Papa," she spoke again to him, "We need to get water. How can you if you're hungry?"

"Let me die, Lira," he finally spoke, but refused to move. The sudden speech shocked Lira, and she nearly dropped the dirt as she fell to her knees, "Let me die and go fetch water yourself."

"But Papa!" she cried, pushing herself closer to him with the dirt in her hand to feed him. He took a feeble hand and slapped hers, sending the dirt scattering across the floor.

"Leave me, daughter of a filthy whore," he repeated while remaining on the earth.

I assure you; Lira's mother was no whore. She had a pure heart, but one day food was scarcer than usual, and so Lira's father killed her mother, cooked her in a pot and piece by piece, they ate her.

Moving on, Lira's heart grew heavy, and she sniveled as wee children did, wiped steaming tears from her face as she scurried across the floor in a darkened corner of the room. Her tummy growled, and she was someone small that needed to move further and further away, ashamed to be related to the man she loved, the one who had genuinely cared for her. I know, not what you'd expect.

Here lies the world, Alkel, their daily lives. Hungry. Thirsty. Hopeless. That soil only satisfies the hunger urges, but it has nothing they need in terms of nutrients. A diet solely built upon rocks is damned to get them all killed. Lira was thirsty that day, and hungry. This is the start of every single day of every single family that lives on the outer most parts of the city, shunned, and pushed out until they die or eat each other alive. Doesn't that just weigh on you?

Do you know what makes this especially dangerous for someone like Lira?

The green orbs decided to light and revealed the roads leading down to the market district, a completely different part of town, one with food and water to spare. But no one was ever kind enough to spare any, regardless of it being a child. In fact, children all alone were often picked up, kidnapped, either eaten or sold for labor or destined to have their identity erased for a life of brothels. Alkel, do yourself a favor, never bed someone from the brothel: could be someone's child.

There it is. Use that bucket. It's what it's there for. I'm going to need it after. Sick world we live in. Truly despicable, and people have the power to do something about—

Different time, same problem, and this time it's around every damned corner.

Imagine a little girl traveling a road as long as that, as dark as that, where she would be seen as a nice piece of meat to eat, produce, or other depraved things. This is your fault. Why don't you change it? Oh, that's right. Sar will kill you before you even have the chance. Lira's so frail, Alkel, what will you do to save her from that? She can only traverse the Abyss, and even that is no small feat for anyone. You know this, for you dare not brave it even with an armored guard at your side.

Mother, Mother, why must you show me this? All I want is to die. Depart me from this world that I may finally know rest.

Part Two

What's that sound?

Alkel? Alkel, wake up! Now is not the time to sleep. Mother, how could you bring me such a frail diminutive boy to tell the tale, the same old tales that repeat under his very nose. What is he to you?

There. Now you're awake. Are you ready to listen?

Good. Now, don't go to sleep. Hey! Stop looking for the door. The way out will remain shut until Mother is done with you. No. Killing me will not open the door. I'm not the one who sealed it shut. Now, you've only one choice: listen to this tale, and take it. You need to vomit? I can't believe you can sleep after the first.

Why am I telling you this? Simple. The story I'm weaving is one of many realities lived by your subjects underneath your feet. You people, foul, morally destitute. You're no better than when the walls first rose up from the earth, scouring the lands underneath the oppressive hell flames scorching the crust of the world. Behold, you bastard!

Poor Lukam. He's a boy, you see, lives on the other end of town, closer to the castle walls you live so peacefully behind, Prince of everything, and yet, Prince of ignorance. Thankfully not of arrogance, you swine. Similar bed to Lira's, nothing special, but his hunger pangs woke him up in what he presumed was the wee hours of the morning.

He rolled off his bed, back cracking, bones brittle, as he stumbled forward in the near blackness. The only light, a lantern, threatened an orange hue illuminating the early dusk, hanging, creaking as a soft wind dared to brush by. He gritted his teeth and stumbling further from the light. His shadow cast a dark path as his gaze peered into the darkened halls, into shades of the room across from his, which was where his mother laid and often slept late.

Stumbling further, he shifted his legs until the darkness embraced his husk, his hands reached for both walls. Each step slid on the cold metal, feeling for each footing, and one by one, he moved his feet cautiously downward to the base of the hovel. He took himself into the common room, tripping over the lip of the barrier between the rest of the house and the corridor, crashing into a chair. Well, what was left of it.

He grimaced; the muscles nearly sprained over the accident. It was almost as if he existed as a cautionary tale, and nothing more. Omnipotence? Or Mother's Sovereignty, praise be Her glorious name! He wrapped his ankle with the sleeve of his shirt, moving toward the kitchen illumined by radiance coming in from outside and he took his candle. Yes, he too had *one* candle. And you, all cozy in your castle, have thousands of candles and torches. Lukam and his mother have one! One! And you cock-waffles can't seem to spare one for someone else? Do you know how much of a luxury it is to have just one candle? Alkel, do you still not understand?

Well, what happened there? I got distracted. You would have too had you the heart for the unnecessary as I do.

What was that, Alkel? You find them necessary? Then treat them like it!

Anyway. Hungry. Thirsty. No food. Sound familiar? So, what was he to do? What was he to do, Alkel? Don't even try to answer that. Your rich ass would just presume, oh, 'why can't he just get it delivered like me?' The answer, because the poor don't have servants, dumbass! So let me tell you what he did.

He climbed up the counter and opened the creaking cupboard, if such a word exists in your vocabulary anymore. Oh, it doesn't? It's a place where you normally put cups. And you'd know that if you didn't rely on servants doing your bidding. After taking the two cups down, he took himself outside. It was dark but the faint glimmer from the lanterns were reaching the back in the thick mud and dung, now coating his shins.

He moved his way through, following the oinking and squealing of the pigs. He pushed his way past them, and he could see the pigs as clear as day. He moved back to the pigs, leaning down, gazing at those beautiful udders as they fed carelessly, and placed both tankards underneath each one, and the pig squealed, moving, nearly tipping over the tankards as he milked her.

Lukam was pushed right over, and had he not instinctively rolled away, he would have been crushed by the mother who had just been robbed of her milk. The young lad kicked the dirt with his feet, just avoiding being crushed, and he scurried around like a rat. Yes, a rat! He turned to the other side of the swine, scooped up the cups of pig's milk, and hurried back inside.

Panting voraciously, he sat himself on a stool, with one cup to his face, and the gamey white substance parted his lips, coating part of his tongue on the way down, refreshing him, and putting his hunger pangs at ease, at least, for the time being. He wiped the white film from his upper lip. He took the full cup of milk, while balancing the candle, which lit his way as he carefully brought his legs over the short barrier he'd tripped on earlier. But that was not all, he could see the steps, the iron steps, rusting on the edges with caked on crimson liquid, days old at this point, with iron pieces and fragments sticking out like sharp blades.

He took several careful steps upward to his mother's room. She had promised to take him to the market on that day to get some food. What day was it? I know not, Mother hasn't revealed it to me. Now, as I was saying before some pig pooker interrupted me, he went into his mother's room, and she was sleeping. He set the candle atop a counter space that had nothing but dust laid upon it. Yes, his mother was naked on the stone slab she rested her body on, but her clothes remained tucked away in the corner. Such a trivial matter. And he placed the cup of milk at the side of her bed, and sat in the middle of the floor, twiddling his fingers as children do. Yes, despite such grim circumstances, never forget, he was but a child.

An unknown time had since passed, and his mother had yet to wake up. The hunger pangs began again, and he was tempted now just to take a draft of milk he stole from a pig, specifically for his mother. He mustn't do that, not if he wants her to be good and strong to take him safely to the market to get some food. He felt his tummy, the ribs seemed frail, and to him, he felt if he pushed his ribs harder, they might swing open like a door.

So, what was he to do? Hungry, no longer thirsty, and that gamy, thin white milk was looking appetizing. And so, he went to wake his mother up instead. He brushed her wiry hair out of her face, her eyes sunken in, her thin face, malnourished. Her eyelids were closed, as were her lips, and he touched her bare, cold shoulders. There was no warmth from her, nor any movement.

"Momma," he spoke to her. And she didn't answer, not a whisper, not even a moan, or a grunt. Nothing. "Momma," he spoke again, with a sharp stilt to his voice. Again, just as you might suspect, no answer. He pushed harder on her this time, and let out an even louder scream, "Momma!" He cried with great tears of sadness; he stood, wiping his face with his sleeve, stamping his feet, and his brittle hands made half closed fists at his side, striking his hips repeatedly as he fell into a tantrum. Poor thing.

As I see from the expression so disgustingly carved upon your face, you already know what happened. She died in the night. Why? You dare ask me why? What have you not been paying attention to? These dismal conditions are left to fester, and those at the bottom, serving, whom your family see not fit enough to lick the dung off their own boots, are left in these hovels, with little food, and less water while you gorge on it like it grows on trees!

Unlike every other foul beast that roams the earth, like every man, Nezkas, or Nezkamen, women, even the children, they're all pitifully weak and unnecessary, but truth be told, this world is too cold, too brutal, and too cruel for one of such purity, such as Lukam's mother was. She was compassionate. She was beautiful, even with a few missing teeth, the scars, and wounds, and the barely manageable frame, so scrawny that a stiff wind might pull her apart.

You see, people are so poor here, Alkel, so destitute. Parents wouldn't think twice about whoring out their children or selling them entirely for a quick coin. But the thought of doing that to poor Lukam never once crossed her mind. You feel, isolated. Your emotions are getting the better of you, Prince Alkel of the Southern Kingdom of this Land of Dreams. Ha! Land of Dreams. That's what we called it when the walls were first raised. Let not your emotions get the better of you, otherwise, you might end up like her. Dead, barren, without a future, and without children, well, maybe one. But let's see first how Lukam fairs then, shall we? Or perhaps, you'd like to take a minute—

Ah, there it is. Aren't you glad Mother made you that bucket? Pleasing to vomit in, I'd rather not have to clean it up afterward. Mother only drinks the finest water, and some life fluid on occasion, only when that would become necessary. Well, do let me know when you're ready to continue.

Part Three

Alkel, stop throwing up, you swine! You'll dehydrate! What am I even saying. Another word lost in translation. You fool. You'll die!

There you go. Get it all out, and don't bother trying to—oh Mother. That stench. That's worse than the time I got eaten whole by the giant only to be removed from his bowels. May it forever be forgotten. Don't ever listen to what your father said. You can forget things that happened to you, but never the sensations. Even if your nose was cut off, certain things might remain.

There, back in your seat? Good, now where were we?

Lukam. Mother is dead, poor thing. And the poor lad was still hungry. What was he to do? Well, first off, let me tell you about the confines, the bowels of the refuse systems that your father loves to perpetuate to keep his subjects sick as dogs, being fed nothing but worms to crawl around through their bellies until nothing but skin, fur, and bones remain. Where do we start exactly?

The marketplace? You see that is where this story will end, at least, for Lukam, anyway, but first, you understand, I must tell you why he must go to the marketplace. Do you care to hear it? No? Well, too bad. You didn't come here to dictate Mother's story. You came here to listen, and now, exposition. Never ideal, but this is necessary. And what I'm about to tell you, even Lukam knows. How is it that a poor peasant beggar of a child knows more than an arrogant, learned prince? Lived experience, rather, second hand lived experience, as his mother, before her passing, told all these things to him, and some he got the unfortunate displeasure of seeing for himself.

Where to begin? Alkel, I think I should start with a place that is close to you, shall I? Or shall I end there and go to the less than admirable place others call Heaven, less they know any visitation to this location is sure to reduce their life expectancy ten-fold. They will be nothing but walking corpses as their empty husks are filled with pleasure and decaying disease. Such visitation drives those who survived such foul places mad to where they feel the worms crawling through their skin and grab the sharpest thing they can find, often a rock, to scrape their skin away and carve themselves to death. Not a pretty sight, if I do say so myself.

Nah, I don't want to distract myself too much, you do that to me enough, vomiting all over the place. Had this been a fucking subway, I'd throw you off.

No, you don't need to know what a subway is.

Down below where you sleep, and further down in the darkened corridors with flames lit by naturally burning metal. Even I know not from where it came, but it burns, it doesn't melt. Wood, after all, is in such short supply. You're literally inside the only tree left! And the bark doesn't peel easily off, Mother allows it not. But persist, and the truth will reveal itself. I recommend you take a trip down there and see the necromancer your father says isn't down there. See for yourself the source the water you all drink. The liquid that produces the grapes on the vine that you may ferment into the perverted version of what someone used to respectfully call wine.

Further down in the dungeons where your father likes to keep his prisoners, and his playthings for some unknown reason, you'll find a place destitute. Chains hold them to the walls, gripping tight against their wrists such that, should you make the effort to examine them, are chaffed with red marks, rendering fingertips white as a bone, less the world finds out what they did. Do you want to know what they did? They murdered for food. They were hungry, Alkel, and they will die chained to those walls, eating nothing but what is handed to them.

Sorry, I couldn't help but find this funny. Handouts? No. Not in this life. Not in this world, for such generosity is plagued with ulterior motives drawn out with the cursed use of man. After all, why would anyone dare part with their food when there is so sparce anyway? Not unless there was a promise, or a risk rather, of getting more food because of it. Alkel, do you know what they eat down there? Do you know what they drink? Rats. The furry, flea infested rats, infected with diseases of their own, plaguing them from within until they're sitting in their own piss and shit. They eat the rats and drink their fluids. That's it. Sounds like a nourishing—

Don't look at me like that. For Mother's sake, Alkel, have some fucking manners. If you don't like it, why don't you implore your father to make a change then, eh? Oh wait, he hates you. Never mind, Desolate Prince of Nothingness. Perhaps if we make a man out of you, perhaps he might change his mind. Fat chance of that with a woman like Sar, worth ten men, that one, perhaps even a few Nezkama here and there. Nah, she's likely to cut off your balls and hang you upside down before cracking your skull open.

Now where was I?

Well, you get the idea now. Getting thrown in prison in exchange for food was not an easy concept to accept. Not for our dear Lukam, anyway. Not for him. Deplorable place, if he went there to get food, the misfortune that would have undoubtedly followed him was being eaten alive. Vore, some like to call it. Or straight up cannibalism. Some people like that sort of thing.

Are you a voraphile, Alkel? Good. It's best you aren't. You've got some sanity and decency about you. Such a tragedy, such despair filled within the world, the saner people prefer just to go about their daily lives and worry about the food on their tables. Others have descended into madness and taken upon themselves the desire of such horrid activities that might make even a devil vomit. Don't be like them, Alkel, I'm going to like you, but not of my own volition, you see, for Mother has imparted that will upon me. That's it and by no merits of your own did you deserve what you have and are going to receive so aplenty if you do what you're told.

Now, where was the other place he could have gone to go get food? Alkel, want to hazard a guess? No? Well, I'd think you might know of such a place as your father tends to frequent it from time to time. Mother tells me he's impotent due to all his unnecessary activities at the brothels.

Oh, yes, the brothels. What? You don't think children find themselves in awe of looking at other men and women dancing with such a sensuous design, with or without their clothes on, oil on their dreadfully scarred skin. Yes, some children go there, and are drawn in with the promise of food. Their fates become so intertwined in disease and tragedy it's absurd. I mean, Alkel, if these things didn't actually happen every day, it would be funny. There are so many ways to go.

Of course, should the brothel's owners get involved with those unfortunate enough to be ensnared by their own desperation, they may kidnap the child and take them up to their personal quarters and train them in the art of sensuality. Pedophiliac bastards. And then, they would raise them up, bring them among the ranks with all the whores under his thumb, and get as much coin as they can with the simple child, whose body and mind were now broken, programmed to know nothing else!

One might have a decent life, trapped, and caged by their new mistress and master, slowly beaten to death. Why? Or with what? Wires, knives, thrown tables and chairs, or even in some cases, hanged outside the window, only to be discarded soon thereafter to be cut up and cooked for tomorrow evening's meal for the patrons that would come up and eat the poor child before fucking the man or woman who killed it.

Another such possibility is a child simply begging for food, and instead of the patron inside said brothel going to bed with one of the men or women, whose job it was to sleep around with any old strumpet or rakehell who asked for it, the child might make a permanent toy for such an adventurer, a knight even, yes, even a knight in these lands will do such a horrid thing, kidnap the child, use and abuse them until there was nothing left, and then succumb the child to self-cannibalism, or eat them themselves.

Tell me, Alkel, which one of these options do you prefer?

None of them, you say? You chose right. And our dear Lukam, was aware of the risks, and would much rather have gone to the prison cell. At least then, it was quick, and excruciatingly painful, or so he imagined. As you can see, neither of these options were on the table for our dear lad, and he was smart, clever enough to know that while the marketplace might not be as viable as he might have liked, the risk of death, torture, or mutilation was substantially lowered, though, not zero.

So, Lukam did what any reasonable person would do. He left his mother there, let her rest peacefully, for he, like his mother, was pure in a world plagued with impurity. He would not defile his mother's body, nor sell her corpse for food, or eat her himself. He let her be, and he wept there, stamping, tears flooding out, rolling them clean with his fists before settling down, his hunger pangs returning after his bout of facing the new reality that was in front of him.

He was but a child. No father, and now his mother was dead, taken in her sleep in the darkness of the night by something so benevolent, I can only imagine Mother did that. Lukam's mother was pure, and so was Lukam. These two people you'll never meet Alkel, you'll not get the privilege to understand who they were, but know that they, and those who are cut of the same cloth of purity who never succumbed to their desires or despair, are few. And when born, they are born terminal for they are not long for this world. Trust me when I say that Lukam's mother was the oldest of such cloth. 'Tis a discouraging thought, don't you think?

No. That was a rhetorical question, you fool. Do not answer it!

Lukam took himself out of the hovel and went to the cobblestone road. Now later in the day, he could see. The lanterns were lit, swaying with the careless wind, and the green orbs in the sky illumined the way for him as he continued pushing his small, brittle legs toward the center of town. The sounds in his ears were the echoing of hundreds of people behind him, and in front of him, and he, alone in a sudden mass of people, human, Nezka, and Nezkama alike, all going to the same place and with the same purpose.

As you might imagine, he found himself to be uncomfortable. Of course, even you would. Picture yourself in it, Alkel. Imagine for just an instant, that your mind was capable of thinking about something or someone other than yourself for once. You're a child. Defenseless. No mother or father to protect you, and not even the communal bond of others his age to help support him. Imagine on either side of you, a Nezkama, hungry for anything that moved, gnashing its teeth, ready to beat you violently to the sod and eat you? Or a Nezka, cruel creatures, just barely taller than the average human, tail whipping about, ready to feast. Or perhaps the murmurs of a group of children behind you, scheming on how to jump you at the advantageous time, and devour you while you were still alive, not that you'd have much meat on your bones anyway. Or a human, man or woman, it doesn't matter what, who'll just knife your throat and be done with it. You wouldn't feel anything, the most merciful way to go.

Can you picture it, Alkel? Just nod, that's all. Good. Because now that you've put yourself in his shoes, you could imagine that all those thoughts and possibilities are what ran through Lukam's mind. He's much smarter than most would give him credit for, but desperation can often dull the sharpness of the mind.

Good, now you're at the marketplace, as he was. I don't think I need to remind you how dreadfully busy it can be, and things might escape your notice, since they all seem to be happenstance whenever, and wherever, you found yourself. You see, Alkel, when a boy is alone, and when they have nothing, they watch things carefully, understanding the frailty of life, and understanding how vulnerable they are. But Lukam was hungry, as hungry as any child would be, after all, he only had the two cups of pig's milk.

He saw a particular stand. It was busy, and a large hulking Nezkama guard who had many scars proving his prowess in battle was defending this particular merchant. You might imagine the scent of the cooking of various meats as the smoke penetrated the air, clouding the green orbs above, and only the flames of some torches of the merchant's stands, and little more than the orange hue it gave off in the crowds of people, shouting, pushing with their coins out, ready to get the first offering of whatever animal this particular merchant was selling.

But one thing was certain, the aroma filled the air, and Lukam was thrust with a lustful heart for this particular beast, driven mad with hunger, though he wasn't without reason. You see, smart as he was, he scurried below the patrons' knees to the stand, prudent to avert any attention from himself. He shifted to the stand, crouching scrupulously.

The crowd was busy, and so too was the merchant negotiating with each patron as they shouted their price for a limb, some fingers, or claws of with whatever it was. What was it, Mother? Not important. His eyes remained fixated on the Nezkama, the tail lashing, his gnarled horns, a grimace on his face, lips barely parting to allow his tongue out, a long spear impaled in the dirt next to him.

Lukam inhaled softly, and his hands reached to the side of the stand. His brittle legs were just tall enough, that he managed to pick some flesh off the side, already conveniently sliced off. Pulling it off, he placed it in his satchel, holey as you could very well imagine, and scurried off back into the crowd, as fast as his legs would carry him. He paid little attention to those around the perimeter of the marketplace, and woe is him.

A firm grip grasped his wrist, and he found himself in the precarious situation, of hanging in the air. A low growl and warm breath entered his ears, you could imagine how notoriously unpleasant that was. I recommend this not.

"Where is it?" the Nezkama growled, "Where is the loot ye stole?"

Lukam swung in the air, grimacing in pain with the grip on his wrist. His other hand let the satchel drop, and he attempted to wring himself free, but the Nezkama, you understand, was much stronger than he. With a whirl, Lukam felt the wind brush past his brittle hair as his arm was being strained, and suddenly, the earth looked a lot closer. His skull nearly cracked open like a pathetic fragile egg, and he felt woozy, vision blurred.

"Where is it?" the Nezkama continued, "Where is the theft ye little runt?"

"I dunno no theft," Lukam replied, and he was ripped back up, hanging there yet again.

"I ain't gonna ask again," the Nezkama said, "Ye ain't got use for a hand, wanna save it, tell me where it is!"

"I dunno," Lukam continued.

"Shit," the Nezkama replied, hurling him down, and stomping on his forearm, nearly fracturing the bone. He could have broken it, you understand, this demon, if you will, yes, yes, I still call them this. What else was I supposed to call them? Their ancestors just walked up from the cracks of the earth, being released from Hell. Of course, that's what they are. The Nezkama grabbed an axe from behind him.

That got Lukam's attention, as you could imagine. He started squealing like a dying pig, "It's in the satchel. The satchel! Don't hurt me please!"

Maybe he should have spoken sooner, or perhaps the Nezkama wanted to play with him first as the axe swung down, hacking into his wrist. The dull blade cracked Lukam's wrist. He tossed, turned, grabbed his hand with the other, but was kicked back down. The Nezkama swung again, and the rusting blade stuck into his flesh, touching the bone, splitting it. He pulled back his swing, and through another, finally severed the boy's hand from his arm, and now, all that remained of the hand was a bleeding stump.

The Nezkama took the severed hand and put it in his own pocket. Grabbing the satchel, he pulled out the meat and walked away, leaving Lukam screaming, trying to bandage up his wound, gore gushing out through the cracks of his fingers—

Mother. Mother. No. Lira. Save Lira. Please, I implore you. Save her and strike down that beast. Strike it down. Not the K'hara. No. I'm begging you. Kill the boy. Kill him. Make him rue the day he did anything like that to her. Kill him, rip him to shreds!

Part Four

Are you serious? Did you just, did you just drop that bucket? Oh, my fucking Mother, Alkel, I can't believe you. Fuck you, you useless piece of shit. I can't believe, gah! You were supposed to vomit in the bucket, not drop your putrid shit all over the place. You're a fucking cunt. There's a special place in Hell for people like you, who pull shit like this. What the fuck, Alkel!

Clean that up.

Now, where was Lira during all—ah, yes, I remember.

She was huddled up in a corner, crying her eyes out because her father just called her mother a whore repeatedly and slapped her wrist like she was a bad wee puppy. A bad little girl. The thought echoed inside the chambers of her mind continuously. Should she hear it often enough, she might start to believe it, but there was one saving grace from all of this, one distraction. Her hunger pangs. Such a dreadful thought, and here I was telling you just how horribly destitute they were and praising it all the same as a distraction.

Such irony, don't you think? Such horribly dreadful things can take the form of a blessing should the occasion call for it. Like in her case. Right there, right then, Alkel. And you think you have it rough, cleaning that—

Oh, Mother. What did you eat? The stench! If I never smell that again, it would be too soon.

Well, as I mentioned before, traveling on the main road is chancy enough as it is, and yet to compel Lira to do such a thing, frail as she was, isolated as she was, vulnerable as she was, how could we be so cruel, Alkel? Especially this early in the morning as those emerald orbs weren't lit up yet. So, how was she to go get food? Obviously, for her, the only place for her to go with any glimmer of hope, you understand, was the marketplace.

Ha. You see where this is going don't you? Two children, indignant, parents seemed to abandon them, one by mere departure from this world, and the other through his utter hopelessness. Lira, though hurt by his actions, loved her father just as much as Lukam loved his mother. And though she was hungry, like Lukam, the thought to eat him didn't cross her mind.

But she remembered her friend Burkam, not to be confused with Lukam, you must understand, two different parts of the town. Their names just so happen to be similar. One could be friendly enough, the other, well, I'd hate to see what kind of man he'd be when he grew up. Dastardly thing. Rotten fruits. Rotten hearts. Almost seems like a tiny version of Sar, now that I think about it.

Oh yes. Shudder, Alkel. You should be shuddering. I wonder what will happen. Hm? Hazard a guess as to how this tale might end. Oh, no. It doesn't quite end that way, though, perhaps the way you just mentioned might have been ideal, given what actually happens. Oh, it gets so, so much worse. Honestly, Alkel, I'm a little disappointed in you. You spend so much time around Sar, and that is the worst you come up with? I almost pity you.

Lira decided to exercise more bravery than you ever dared, than you ever could. Plenty courage in one measly finger she had than an entire group of guards trained to protect you. What did she do, Alkel? What else was she to do but vault through the window toward the back of her house, landing her legs into the Abyss. The Abyss, Alkel. So many things happen in the Abyss, the perpetual black aura of dark and cold, brings chills to my bones just thinking about it. You too? Well, I don't have a spare cloak for you to borrow, so just deal with it.

You could imagine her fright, the bones inside her frail, hungry body just shaking in the cold dark, and her eyes averted to the sky, completely black. She couldn't even see her hovel anymore as she stepped further into it. It was almost like—taking a plunge into cold water, far too cold for your liking. But unlike water, which when you're in allows your body to adapt to its temperature, this cold remains with you.

She descended further into the dark, an unknown sludge caked her legs with each step. She moved forward, getting further and further away from her hovel. She heard a screech. Yes, yes. That's it. A K'hara! A great beast flying in the air, and unlike traditional animals, they can see in the Abyss. They care not for the light. Another reason to flock to the light during such times, don't you think? But it was too early, and she had traversed too far for that to be an option.

She gritted what remained of her broken teeth. The sludge was heavy on her legs, but she persevered, her heart pumping and pounding as she felt the earth ascending to the sky, closer to the screeching. Covering her ears, she glanced further into the dark, hoping against hope that the green orbs were lit, or that she'd happen upon the lantern swiveling in front of Burkam's hovel before it was too late. But such luck was in such short supply, well, for most people anyway.

For she kicked an unseen object, bruising her shin. She flipped over onto the ground, more mud, and she could hear the pig's oinking and squeals. She wiped the sludge from her face and the screeching K'hara, though now distant still cast cold wind down with the flapping of its wings, and the pigs started moving further away from the fence she tripped over. She beheld the aura of light, swiveling in the dark in front of a hovel. Burkam's hovel, and so with her bruised shin, her heart racing, palms sweating, no doubt, she ran to the lantern to take a deep breath and allowed the warm rays of light to cascade her filthy body.

Shivering underneath the new sensation of warmth, you could imagine she hugged herself as tightly as her weak, frail arms could. The orange hue cascaded over her, and the sludge dripped away, the dung pile, and the vitality, and other foul things that misshapenly found themselves caught in the Abyss. The blackness that is unknown except for the risk of light. It's unsafe.

You know this to be true. Especially when the K'haras are out at night.

I want you to imagine yourself in perpetual blackness. No, you cannot see the outlines, or silhouettes, oh, yes, the Abyss is that dark. Imagine the chills scouring through your bones and skin and imagine the strength leaving your body. Pair that with the sudden screeches of the K'hara, and you find yourself all alone, forever in the dark. Do you now picture yourself in her shoes, Alkel? Good. Now, how vulnerable do you feel?

Is she safe? Not yet. Well, perhaps for the time being, but she hadn't made it to Burkam's hovel just yet: is anywhere really safe? It's right in front of her, ha! She gazed upon the hovel at the other end of the path leading to it, another lantern to signal the entrance, and the iron slab was kicked open, half swinging on one hinge. The creaking slab was like someone drove a knife in your ear. Not pleasant at all. Not. One. Bit.

She saw faint shadows inside. A table, some counter space, some chairs, a pot in the middle, hung up by some rods, and a fire pit for some burnable metal. She carefully removed herself from the safety of the lantern's light, walking slowly inside the hovel, and her footsteps, moved gingerly upon the ground, breaking through the threshold of Burkam's home.

Startled, a noise creaked from the side where the dark hall was, leading to the stairs to the bedding quarters. A light flared down, glimmering on the metal, slowly approaching footsteps. She put her hands up, nonchalantly, like this, as the person with the light revealed themselves. A woman in her mid-thirties. I'm surprised she managed to live that long myself. Hairs of wire on her head, just like Lira's, and who could forget naught but the breaking of the teeth, as she opened up, an awkward smile, if you could imagine, a curious tongue licking through the toothless holes where teeth used to be. Eyes sunken into her thin face, like her father's, but far be it for me to ignore, malnourished as she was, weak was not one of them. She was strong, and able. Her strength was endearing, and then she opened her mouth.

"Whatcha doin' 'ere?" she asked. Yes, Alkel, believe it or not, their speech often is broken.

Frightened, Lira stammered, fumbling her words, as you could very well imagine at the sudden sharp, and unwelcomed tone Burkam's mother presented her with. "I want ta play with Burkam."

"He sleepin'," his mother growled. "Too ear'y. Go back home."

His mother walked around her and shifted her eyes to the kitchen as the light lit the room. Mud tracked in through outside, a pile of dung, I think that's what that is, shifted out in the corner with several rat tails squirming about. She took her hand in the dung pie, ripped out a squealing rat, and brought it close to her face as she set the candle down.

She sat herself down on a chair, glaring at Lira as she pet the rat with a boney finger. It stopped moving, and her wrist wrapped around the neck, twisting it with a loud crack. The rat was no more, and she brought the furry breakfast to her face, her mouth wide open. Broken teeth entered the weak hide of the rat. Blood scoured, pouring on her chin as she chewed the rat, eating what little meat it had on its bones. Chewing up and down, an aroma of life water reached Lira's nose, and her tummy growled again.

Lira licked her lips with hunger, and slowly walked forth to Burkam's mother, asking politely, with two open hands like a bowl, yes, like this, "May I have one?"

"No! Mine. Get. Get out! Burkam sleepin'!" she growled, immediately moving to her dung pie trap with the squirming rat tails. She grabbed a rusting knife from the counter and pointed it at Lira. "Get yer own. Yer own food. Not mine. Not Burkam's. Get out!"

"But it's dark outside, can't I wait until Burkam wakes?" Lira asked reasonably, but as you could imagine, Burkam's mother was none too reasonable. Ha. How reasonable could an old hag be if she would dare raise a knife to a defenseless little child, frightened that even a child could take away what scarce food she had, smothered in dung.

Well, Lira had no choice. She dropped her hands to her side, and turned herself away from Burkam's hostile mother, who still scampered with blood on her lips, and rat flesh stuck between what few teeth remained in her mouth. She skirted off from the darkness in the hovel and placed herself underneath the same old lantern yet again, waiting for Burkam to awake, or his mother to leave for the day. So, she sat across the path with her back touching the Abyss, and she felt like a cold, dying finger was brushing up against her. Such fear, Alkel. Can you imagine it?

Are you done cleaning up your filth yet? Good. Now, ha, we can get to the good part. The part with some conflict, rather. Such conflict in a world in which conflict is normal and justified most of the time. But soon, Alkel, you'll see just how rotten the people of this world are.

Part Five

Alkel! Gah. What the Hell. Is wrong with you? Shit. That's gonna leave a mark. Do you have any idea how hard it is to replace this cloak? The material doesn't just pop out of nowhere. Resources are finite, a word too old for your wee brain—

Now, what. Don't you dare. Alkel. You son of a bitch! See! See all the nothing that did. No, that axe will not penetrate the hide of the tree. You want out? Well, maybe if you didn't interrupt me every so often, my tale would be done, and the door open. That is Mother's tree. Her precious, the bark is hard and firm just like her older brother used to be, olden in his years, sure, but sadly, no more. But you didn't come here to—

Mother compelled you here to be adopted. That's why you're here, and now, you must listen to my story, even if it kills you. It would be best for everyone if you just died. Mother, can I hang him? No? Fine. Alkel, take back your seat, and I swear, don't you dare dump your vomit on the soil again. Mother deserves more care and respect than that.

Okay, now where were we—ah. Lira and Burkam.

She was outside, staring at the empty husk of a hovel, and hours passed, and the green orbs started to light the sky, filling her with a sense of ease as the Abyss retreated as Abysses do when confronted with a violent light. Some steps entered her ears, and she looked down the path, now visible as the path was no longer infested with the Abyss, and any threats of K'hara were nulled by the threat of light, thankfully. Terrible business. Nezkas, Nezkamen, men, women, children walked along the path, moving this way and that, filling the road. There was one such group of people that caught her attention though, perhaps less innocent than others, I know, but you might imagine.

There was a man, leading a group of children, his children, they had his eyes, but they too had their fair share of malformities. Could you imagine the skin and bones, picturing the rot in their bellies as they struggled to move? The father staggered, dropping on his knees, and Lira heard the impact of his head to one of the loose cobblestones. Gore bleeding from a crack in the skull.

One of his older children, a girl, perhaps your age, frail and weak, rummaged through the man's bags and pulled out a knife, rubbish, rusting, of course, in what other condition would you expect to find a knife of eating? She cut into his flesh, ripped his ligaments, and handed bits and pieces of his body to her siblings, and they ate, gleefully, laughing and playing, dancing, prancing like the joyful idiots they were, butchery dripping down their chins. Yes, whoever she was, she wasn't foolish, for she offered bits and pieces to others as they passed by in exchange for some coin. It was her father after all, why not—

Damnit Alkel, what did I say about interrupting!

So, why would she not take advantage of his sudden weakness? If it was her who was dead, she'd share the same fate. Survival of the fittest at its finest, Alkel, isn't it glorious? Her siblings, herself included, were fed, and she had coin in her pockets. But for how long, well, she'll have another story filled with tragedy, I'm sure. Perhaps her younger brother will scheme for it. Who knows. Or maybe she'll toss him up to the rats and see how he likes it.

I seem to have gotten a bit off course here, you'll forgive me. You've no choice, so Lira observed this, and looked passed to the doorway again, huddling herself to the lantern, holding it tight, since she was now vulnerable to those around her who would look at her as a delicious morsel. Ironic, don't you think? The roads are perilous at night as you travel the Abyss. The roads are equally treacherous during the day, only this time, they have other troubling matters, especially for Lira.

Well, Alkel, in any case, it might be prudent for me to suggest that Burkam's mother has since left the hovel, and Lira scurried the echoing cobblestones, careful of any wandering eyes that might view her as being isolated enough to take with them, with minimal risk. She was, after all, alone in this world, especially now since her father had taken so marginal an interest before even acknowledging her existence.

Why, do you think, Alkel, he did that? Care to guess why?

Eh, not quite. As I've already seen how this tale unfolds, it will be apparent enough why he did what he did, and you yourself, unless you are irredeemably stupid, will know why. It should be made obvious, in a world so dark and murky, that whether your left hand is, in fact, attached undoubtedly to your left wrist, well, we could all split hairs on the difference between them, but you couldn't tell the distinction.

She went inside. The furniture was well enough out of the way that she made her way to the eating area, and took herself upon a stool and waited for Burkam to wake. Fortunately, it was late enough in the day that she heard footsteps echoing off the halls from the corridor leading to the stairs up the second floor, and he peered around the bend. Like his mother, he wasn't weak. He even had muscle on his arms. Not a year older than Lira, I dare say, and he might have had some favorable feelings toward her. Young love, as they would call it.

He yawned, rubbing the sleep from his eyes.

"Lira," he said, "What ye doing he'e so early?"

She looked over at him, leaning against the tabletop, weak hands propped up against her chin, staring with a tear drooling out of her eye. One of her fingers twitched ever so lightly as he walked his way over to her, and wrapped an arm around her shoulder, before swiftly leaving her again to raid the cupboard, pulling some chairs around so he could climb them.

"I'm lonely," she finally answered amid the silence filled with the squealing of the chairs on the floor. "Papa isn't feeling well."

"I understand," he climbed down. "Wait here."

He left the room, vaulting outside to the back of the hovel, and not soon after did she hear the sudden screaming pigs outside. Shortly after, he came back with two tankards of milk. He sat down with her on the other side of the table and slid one her way. She looked at it hungrily, seeing the faint white substance splashing about from inside. She licked her chapped lips. Her two hands grabbed hold of the tankard, firmly but gently, as you normally would when holding a newborn baby. Not that you know anything about that. She brought it to her lips, and allowed the warm milk to sooth her mouth, entering inside it, and she allowed the taste to savor as she swished it through her mouth, before letting it go down her throat and into her tummy.

She felt refreshed, and they talked quite a bit. Turns out, Burkam's mother isn't much too kind. Such a stark contrast to Lukam's mother. After all, Lukam's mother was kind, soft, and beautiful. Burkam's mother, the exact opposite, fearful about her next meal, strong, rough around the edges, and, of course, ugly. She had a face only a mother could love, but even her mother, I fear would run from it. It's a surprise that Burkam stuck around e'en this long.

I won't bore you with mundane details, so I'll go ahead and skip to the marketplace. The two of them, that is to say, Lira and Burkam, sat on a large boulder just on the outside the perimeter. They were high enough that, though the dark was vast, they could see the comings and goings of all the people from inside the market. The tall Nezkama, and their human sized ancestors, Nezka, and humans mingling about trying to purchase goods, or looking for wares to steal.

Every day, you might imagine, someone gets killed here. You wonder who it will be today? But of course, I already know the answer.

"Burkam," Lira said, rubbing her growling tummy, "I want some food. Couldn't we have had some of your rats instead?"

"Nay," he said, leaning back, waiting for an interesting occurrence to happen. An odd pastime for children, don't you think? "Ma would find out. She always finds out when a rat goes missing."

"Well," she said, leaning back with her arms crossing her chest, "the tournament is coming soon. Lots of food to go around."

Of course, what she means by that, is the knight's tournament, right around the corner. That hasn't happened quite yet. I think it's about a fortnight off from tonight. But the tournament, a battle of knights to the death or defeat by serious maiming, she wasn't curious about. Life was so horrible, why would she want to expose herself willingly to uninteresting violence? No, what she was after, were the crumbs that would be discarded by the mouths too uncivilized to chew properly.

"Aye," Burkam agreed, "But we need food today. No promise that Ma will cook anything."

She addressed her tummy, and was considering grabbing another handful of dirt, when Burkam was suddenly excited. He jumped up with glee, his back straight, and he stamped his feet rapidly, pointing into the crowd, "Lira, look! A little boy pulled more than he could chew!"

Lira looked in the direction of the pointed finger, and she heard screaming. A crowd made a circle around a Nezkama guard, and within the circle, a boy was on the ground, struggling to get free, that was, until the axe fell. Once. Twice. The hand came off, and he screamed some, and darted into the crowd, until all that remained unhidden, was the trail of red tracks he left behind. Lira jumped at that sudden excitement, fraught with the tragic realization of mortality.

The boy still lived, with the turmoil of a bleeding stump. Lira knew, as with most people she encountered whenever she ventured off to places where she was, that despite how crafty people were, it didn't matter. Hunger drove people mad, even to the effect that, in this boy's case, they do and take things that they otherwise wouldn't have. It was a risk, and he paid for it.

"Oh, so close. I was rooting for 'im too," Burkam said, as if this was all just some twisted game. Only with this game, people kill one another for food, and not for sport. "Let's go find him."

"What? Why? I thought we was lookin' for some food?"

"We a'e, Lira," he said. "But I've an idea."

The two children looked at the Nezkama who took some meat from the satchel that had since been discarded. He walked back over to a bustling merchant's stand. This stand was busier than all the rest, and even Lira, could smell the delicious food coming from it and she wanted it, plagued with an uncontrollable desire to have whatever it was he was cooking. Given the circumstances of Lukam's and Lira's upbringing, Alkel, I assure you, these merchants didn't waste meat, they preserved it with salt, at least, those that didn't sell that day, which was itself a rarity. She licked her lips and placed a pinky finger in the side of her mouth, blushing at the thought of having some of that delicious food. You must understand, Alkel, you get meat every day, cooked and seasoned meat. When the prospect of such a catch comes across their nose, they can't help but salivate like a mangy mutt. Don't blame me for this. I had nothing to do with the food scarcity, or the lack of cooking skills in the world.

"So, 'ere is what we'll do," Burkam began. "We find him, we can still sco'e the same place, and, assuming the worst doesn't happen, we all get ta eat today."

"What's the plan?" Lira asks, inquisitive now. Burkam was older, not by much, but stronger too, and therefore he held her confidence. Whatever the plan was, she would accept it wholly. Probably a bad way to go about life, especially when the other person knows he has your respect, and your infatuation. Hard not to take advantage of those qualities.

He explained the plan. Lira was to hide by the side of the stand, in the shadows, but not in the Abyss, that would be atrocious. This other boy would provide some form of distraction for the Nezkama guard, and lead him far away. Meanwhile, Burkam, strong as he was, was going to make a commotion, push the crowd into the stand, and in the confusion, Lira would steal some of the food from across the counter. Simple enough plan, right? What couldn't possibly go wrong? Well, perhaps if they didn't rely on a boy with a stump, things might have gone off without disaster.

Burkam led Lira down into the marketplace as they followed the trail of blood into the crowds, and finally, so far away, and near the other end of the marketplace altogether, toward the main road to where Lukam's hovel was. He might consider questioning his own morals, maybe, perhaps he might cave, and just nibble a finger for a while. They found him, his hand covering his stump. He ripped off a piece of his tunic and wrapped it around the stump as secure as he could, looking at them like a terrified little puppy. You know, the look of a puppy who doesn't know he did wrong, but knew the master was going to whip him until the orbs no longer lit and the legs broke?

"What ya want?" Lukam asked.

"You're gonna go far, kid," Burkam said, all smooth like. The boy had charisma, given his age, and knew enough about the inner workings of people to get them to do what he wanted. We used to call that 'psychology' back in my day. Yes, that is who Burkam is.

"I don't—I don't feel like I'll get far," he replied, completely despondent from the reality of the danger he was in. Ha!

After all, with him like this, Burkam and Lira could just kill him themselves and eat him for their meal today. Such precarious livelihoods, and need I remind you as you seem rather perplexed, it isn't new. But let me remind you of your sister. Rach. Imagine Lira as Rach. Don't lose sight of that. For this is her story as much as it is Lira's. They're of the same age bracket after all.

"You took a piece of the meat," Burkam began to explain, while, Lira went to sit next to her new friend, leaning against him to provide some comfort to his ailing body. Such a kind gesture, don't you think? Certainly not one you'd expect in your high and mighty castle where everyone, including your own family, hates you and would rather see you dead. "Nezkama have a smell," Burkam theorized. He just assumed, correctly, I might add. "Unlike any other. You need more than one person to get wares from *that* stand. Let's work together."

He repeated his plan. Told him everything, though the risks he needed not mention. They were implied, as with all things in this life. Now, before you doze off again, Lukam protested, silently of course, they need not let everyone know what they were up to through poor acting. But, for his protest, could you exactly blame him, Alkel? I can't. He just had his hand chopped off; you could imagine he was none too eager to try again. He thought the risks of the brothels, or the prison cells were much better than this. But Lukam was hungry.

And so, without much deliberation or rebuttal, Lukam reluctantly decided to play his role, and he scoured for rocks; his one hand and unsteady body would hurl when the time was right to distract the Nezkama. Not a fair deal if

I do suggest myself. Lira set herself behind the stand, and Burkam off to the side, a path, perhaps one which they would elect to run should things go awry, which is almost a certainty in this accursed Land of Dreams.

All three of them were in their pre-appointed locations. Lukam was set up in the vicinity of the crowd, ready to hurl some rocks at the Nezkama who stole his hand. The bleeding stump was still dripping through the rag as it was saturated with his own vital essence, puddles of crimson lay within the cracks of the cobblestones; you could very well imagine it, and he took it upon himself, once he saw Burkam and Lira in their designated locations, he hurled a rock with force. Unfortunately, he missed the first one, but it caused a ruckus. He chuckled as the rock rattled against the cobble stones behind the Nezkama, who diverted his attention to the sound. Lukam hurled another rock and struck the cretin in the back of the head, who screamed, turning back at Lukam with a scowl upon his face.

Lukam turned immediately and ran, hoping to disappear from the Nezkama's sight, but it wasn't too long before he heard the cretin scavenging the area, pushing other patrons violently this way and that. Others screamed as broken bones were made by those who struck cobble stones in the commotion. He disappeared for quite some time, and now, I'd like to turn your attention to Lira, the sweet little girl who started this dreadful story.

She was behind the stand. Burkam, with the merchant's guard out of the way, hurled his body at the mass of customers at the stand, pushing them into it. The merchant was startled, and he shook his head, shouting profanities into the air, directed at no one in particular. The store owner grabbed the axe hanging on the back of his stand and started hacking away at his customers. The blood, limbs, and severed fingers scattered, providing just enough chaos to ensure that Lira could reach up and pull a significant chunk of meat from the stand, stuff it in her satchel and scurry off like a rat into the mass of people, disappearing to their predetermined location. She squatted just outside the perimeter of the marketplace, hiding behind some iron bushes and some rocks, off the side of the cobblestone path thatt was uncomfortably close to the Abyss.

She waited a significant amount of time for Burkam to arrive. Yes, Alkel, this seems to be going so smoothly. A plan almost too perfect, and yet, somehow, everything went according to plan, for Burkam arrived to Lira's hiding place without incident. They both were hungry. They were not completely insensitive to life, not yet anyway. Well, for Burkam it's forever debatable. They waited though not too long, for the orbs in the sky were dimming and the people of the marketplace started exiting en masse.

As you might imagine, Lira wondered what happened to poor Lukam. Did the Nezkama finally get to him? Burkam wanted to leave, but Lira insisted they wait, and so Burkam relented, frustrated as he was. After all, what could he do after she threatened to throw their hard-earned meal into the Abyss. She would do it. She knew how to be hungry.

Permit me to tell you what happened to Lukam, meanwhile. He dashed through the crowds, weaving this way and that, scuttering through the merchants' stands, which the Nezkama wasted no time ripping to shreds, likely killing anything or anyone that stood in his path to finally kill Lukam. After all, he was suffering now from a terrible headache. The Nezkama tracked him down to the edge of the marketplace, but Lukam knew that he had to get rid of the Nezkama before he returned to his friends.

So, what was he to do? Well, nothing else, except to traverse the black wall of the Abyss, and so he hurled himself into the great unknown. Of course, without fear, driven by rage, the Nezkama followed, the earth shaking underneath the weight of those impressive strides. Some say the eyes of the Nezkama can pierce through the darkness. They theorize this as the Nezkama experience, and what humans wouldn't give for that. They can see in the dark, but not the Abyss, for it is a complete, and total black. It's supernatural. No Nezkama gaze can pierce through its veil. They can smell their way through it, but then, only I know this to be a fact. You'll find nothing of this in books.

Lukam strode himself, weaving this way and that, attempting to deceive the Nezkama, but to no avail. Now, of course, Lukam had since lost his own way, and just strode himself as fast as he could with the muck of whatever his shins stepped in. The ground trembled as it does, and his ears churned inside as the unwelcomed squeal of a K'hara and the flapping of its wings soared above him.

He noticed a light, brief, a small dimming light of a lantern swiveling on a familiar cobblestone. Might not help him lose the Nezkama set on killing him, but the K'hara, maybe he'd get lucky, and it would swoop down and kill the Nezkama for him. As I said, he was no stupid boy, just desperate. And so off he went in a sprint, panting heavily, and he looked down as he passed the threshold of the light, seeing Burkam and Lira glancing at him. Lira smiled with a relief, but Burkam knew better, and pushed her down, and they turned to the cobblestone, and the iron bush, hiding.

Lukam turned briefly, and the Nezkama pursued him, screeching with a half-raised axe, and swung it down with force, just barely missing the boy. Thank you, Mother. The axe struck the cobblestone, and he beheld a crack in the blade. But he knew he couldn't hope to beat the Nezkama, he was just a boy, axe or no axe, and so he braved the Abyss one more time. He fell into perpetual black, crawling in the sludge until he touched an iron bush.

"Come out, boy," the Nezkama growled, "I'm not going to hurt you. I'm only going to chop your damned head off. See how you likes it!"

Lukam heard the loud sniff in the air. It was only a matter of time, and he covered his mouth, one finger stuck between his teeth to prevent them from chattering against one another like horse's hooves. He heard the loud footsteps, and the uncomfortable screams of the K'hara.

Suddenly, a hard projectile was hurled from the other side of the cobblestone road. It struck Lukam in the head. He winced, and the rock rattled as he let out a gripe of pain.

"You!" The Nezkama found him, grabbed his wrist out of the dark, and hurled him into the light.

The force of the fall permitted Lukam's ankles to strain as he struck his head against the cobblestone. His vision faded, and he saw Burkam pulling Lira, who was weeping, into the Abyss, following the cobblestoned road. But Lukam couldn't be bothered with that now, not as the Nezkama drooled over him, his foot on his chest.

"Stupid boy," he growled, axe raised with two hands.

Don't you dare turn away, Alkel, not from this!

The Nezkama brought the axe head down and Lukam's neck cracked as blood poured from both sides of his lips. The Nezkama kicked the dull end of his axe with his foot, and Lukam's head rolled off. In a fit of rage, then he kicked Lukam's head into the Abyss, and dragged Lukam's corpse into the dark, to feed him to his own family.

Part Six

Yes, yes, Lukam is now dead, thanks to you.

Yes, thanks to you. No. He elected to go to where he went. He went on to trust Burkam and Lira. His actions got him killed. But, why don't we take a look at the bigger picture, shall we? You splurge yourself sick, you, Sar, Rach, and Borto, and you all live in comfort, completely ignorant of the rampant hunger your subjects have, encouraging voracity. You have these huge store houses, for what? Food to go bad quickly, rotten, and then discarded into the animal feed. But Lukam never had a chance. He was hungry. Destitute. And now, dead. Because you refuse to lift a finger, sluggard, and he's dead. So many people die like this. Lukam is dead. He is just one unfortunate casualty in all your laziness and blindness.

What are you—Alkel? No burning the tree with my lantern, Alkel. Fine. See what it does.

See. Look at all the nothing that did. Now I have to replace that. Not cheap to make those things, you know. You owe me a lantern. Oh, don't give me that. You've plenty to spare in your castle!

Well, we're about to come full circle, now. Alkel, this is exciting. Allow me to gloss over some details of what happened after Lukam met his untimely demise. Yes, as you might be able to tell, it was Burkam who threw the rock, allowing him and Lira to escape. How could he see them as they moved from the light into the opaque Abyss? It's a supernatural darkness. You physically can't see anything *inside* it. If there is light, just outside the Abyss, you can see that, and the space it illumines.

So, what happened next? They safely traversed one Abyss into the next, sprinting in between orbs of orange lights lit up by the periodically set lanterns across the road, and they made it, safely, to Burkam's hovel. Of course, now, it being night, the orbs in the sky light up space considerably less, and what they have to walk through are small spaces of light, sanctuaries, if you can understand. This is why one doesn't usually travel at night. Unless of course, one has a lantern or a torch.

Lira sat at the eating table in relative quietness as Burkam took the meat, brought it to the counter and cut it into pieces. He started the fire in the center of the room, a hanging pot, and put the meat in it, and it slowly cooked. Upon completing, he portioned it out in thirds, one for them to eat right now, and one for Lira and her family, and one for his. See, even children can be civil.

They ate together, well before his mother got back from whichever brothel she had spent her day in. Oh, you ought to know, she's a part time mistress. She eats there, rarely takes any back for Burkam, hence why he has to do shit like this! The children didn't talk much, but what Burkam did to Lukam, getting him killed like that, it was bothering her as she chewed on the food, unable to find the taste in it, as Lukam should have been able to enjoy it with them. He was their friend after all.

Oh, trust can make you do terrible things, especially when you know the person has no chance. Yes, Alkel, welcome. You know this as much as anyone. You have the same predicament. Servants, guards, family, none of them you trust. You're wise for that. Lukam wasn't so lucky, rather, he had one thing you didn't, well, ha, not right now: Desperation.

Well, moving on, shall we. Lira has to get home after all. So, she left with her bag containing her portion. She was given a candle to take home with her so that she might traverse the Abyss without incident. She took little steps over the cobblestones; the candle lit her way, and she traversed the Abyss with only the light parting the way. There was no incident. Only the K'hara fly at night, no other creatures. Other such animals that would dare be airborne know not to share the same skies as those dreadful birds.

There was a sound in the air that filled her precious ears that keep even the K'hara away. As you know, rarely can you ever trust rainfall, and this incident was no exception. The clouds screeched, and the rain poured down. The feeling against her skin was hot and she, though in between two Abysses, was in the dark again with the candle snuffed out. She discarded it, and threw the bag of meat over her head, bringing her legs up to the air, strode as fast as she could.

The rain dripped down and smoke came up from the earth. The water, wet, and hot it was as it ran down her legs, splashing on her tunic, and her trousers started to burn. Yes, the acid in the air was burning everything away and she screamed in agonizing pain. She felt it searing her flesh as the threads of her tunic started to come undone, and she felt the weight of the acidic water on her bag, seeping through it, peeling the skin away off her precious fingers.

She continued to run, and the holes in her tunic and trousers became exceedingly apparent. And soon, the red swelling started with the peeling of her skin. She mustn't stop. She can't stop. That would mean certain death, and the death of her papa, no less, for what else would he eat? Nothing. He'd barely chewed anything.

She made it to her hovel, rather the end of the road, and you can imagine the steam piling atop her after traversing several Abysses. The skin on her legs, her forearms, her fingers and toes, it was all peeled off, bubbling like hot water. Ha. She strode to a sprint, tripping over her clumsy feet, and struck her cheek against a cobblestone, and the satchel she held the meat in was hurled into the doorway, sliding off in the dark. Still in pain, and now with a swollen cheek, she pulled herself up, and took her body inside.

She struggled in the dark, but do you know what the first thing that she did was, Alkel? Don't look at me like that. I want you to answer. What was the first thing she did? Not quite. The acid started to eat through her clothes so she threw them off her, hurried into the place you might call a kitchen, and grabbed some washcloths, wiping the water off her body, peeling excess of her skin. She was going to have lots of scarring, no doubt about that.

Just imagine it, Alkel, Rach in that poor state of affair. Hungry. Skin, and bones, and now, skin marred, a bruise on her face, and yet, still thirsty. Fortunately, she drank some of Burkam's pig milk before the end of the day, and before leaving his hovel. Such a disaster, don't you think? But at least she still has that meat in her bag, and she rushed to it, rapidly pulling out the meat, and stuffing it into a pot, lighting the fire underneath it, and warminig herself as it cooked. It was already cooked, but now contaminated, if you happen to be wondering why Lira cooked it a second time.

She saw the wounds on her arms, red marks where the flesh was now open for all to see, red bubbles boiling from underneath her skin where the flesh was now exposed. It stung. If I could compare it to something that you'd have any firsthand experience towith it might be akin to listening to one of the new servants scream as your father brands him or her with a red-hot iron poker. Yes, you can imagine the pain she was in, but driven by necessity, she could forgo the agony. After all, it would still be there when she was done.

The acid rain dripped and dropped outside, creating puddles outside, rippling in the pale light barely reaching her front door. She looked outside a moment, wondering where her papa was. Oh yes, you didn't forget about that beggar yet, did you? I hope you didn't. We're about to come full circle, and then some more. He wasn't there, but as she looked out on the other end of the cobblestone street, the lantern swayed, and the smoke from the burning cage rose, shedding the light, and she could see past where the green orbs were as the light of the flames cast themselves further.

The orb is really just a glass ball with a flame inside it, but with no magic during the night. The light itself dims during this time of day, and just past that, perhaps about another three kilometers, was the first layer of black clouds. Now, past those clouds are the truth, the light, the moon, the stars, and the sun! Mother created them, Alkel, she created all of them. We created those blasted clouds that won't allow us to see Mother's creation. Praise her glorious name! Praise her, Alkel. She alone is worthy to be praised! On your knees!

Sorry about that. I can get carried away when I think of all the things Mother has blessed us with, and that we cursed ourselves with darkness to be forever parted from her. Such a trivial matter, regrettably. Now, I must move us back toward the topic, yes? Mother won't like it if I keep you here longer than necessary. After all, we're coming to one conclusion, but Lira's story continues.

Much later in the evening, when the meat was cooked, and tucked away in the kitchen, and the embers moved around the burning metal, still lighting outside, she was finally about to give up, being tired as she was, exhausted, jaded beyond anything you could imagine. You see, Alkel, you barely work. Why would you? You don't know true exhaustion. Your servants even, sometimes are afforded a break here and there, but what of the peasants beneath you and the beggars? They work the fields, pointlessly, I might add, and light the forges for hours, with small amounts of rest, but perhaps in the week, they might get a day off, or two. These people, every waking moment is a span of time spent working, and their reward, another day in Hell.

She took herself to the stairs, carefully looking down at her feet so she might not stumble in the dark. She reached through the doorway and pulled herself into the black. Constantly berated by the sound of the rain on the earth, and hammering against the hull of her hovel, she was annoyed to say the least. But there was one sound that got her attention and drew her mind to a sense of alarm. After climbing three steps, she turned, taking herself down the stairs carefully, and peeked out from the doorway to see the silhouette in the dark, the light glimmering on the face of a man she recognized.

The beggar, Alkel, in the state you'd recognize him. His nose missing, his fingers swollen, and one hand, completely cut off! All he did was ask you for the bread, and you! He wouldn't have been like this if you acted on your compassion. Yes, yes, you saw him for what he was, a human, like you, and for once in your life you felt a certain way, an urge to help someone other than yourself. Your heart strings were pulled and ripped apart of your old self, and here you are, trapped, condemned by the Mother who pulled them. She is your Mother now, Alkel, and you, like me, will serve her to atone for your sins until the day you hang. Let us not forget the story, shall we?

Lira's father stumbled inside, clamoring on the floor. Groaning back, the blood pooled around him, and of course, the skin peeling ever so slowly off his body as the acid rain began to eat away at him like a parasite. Here he lay, and of course, Lira sought nothing more than to help him, so she dashed from out of the doorway to approach him.

"Don't. Touch. Me. Lira," he spoke sharply, and then his voice dropped low, and a soft loving voice came out from the dissonance. "Lira, I'm covered in acid, don't touch me."

"Papa, I have some food," she said, urging him to eat as she went to the corner of the kitchen and pulled out some pieces of the morsel.

"Lira," he said, "come here with a knife."

And so she did. She returned to where he lay with a knife in hand and, of course, the food for him to eat. She took some pieces of meat and held it out to him, and he stared at it hungrily, steam coming off his body as the rain seeped further and further into him. His entire body trembled as he was being eaten away.

"Give me the knife, Lira, you keep that," he said, "Just the knife."

"Papa?" she asked, tilting her head, confused as to what he intended to do with it. But she handed it to him nonetheless.

Taking the knife firmly in his hands, he turned the handle to her, and grabbed it with both hands, the blade pointing at his chest. He panted, heavily. I couldn't be certain if it was from exhaustion, fear, or the amount of pain he was in, or some devilish combination of the three. Yes, Alkel, were you so naive to think only you felt these things? The emotional tugs on your heart are what brought you here to begin with. Yet, you might imagine with the love inside Lira's heart, how troublesome this was as tears flowed down her cheeks.

"Kill me, Lira," he said.

"Papa," she whined, "No."

You see, she shook her head, putting her hands firmly at her side. Eyes closed, but her fingers were trembling. She already lost her mother. She lost Lukam, as small of a part on her life he played, she lost him, nonetheless. How could she bear to lose her father as well, and then, to only have Burkam. Oh, yes. You're quite right to shiver. Such tragedy and an unnecessary display of violence and distrust through the world, one can't live in fear alone, but, for those of them who did, they often lived longer.

"Lira," he pleaded, "This world is cruel. I cannot—I cannot supply your needs anymore. Kill me. Chop me up. Cook me. Eat me. Sell my flesh for coin so that you may have the start of a life I never had."

Why doesn't he just kill himself then? Oh, you'll see.

"Nay, Papa!" Lira pleaded, turning her gaze to his. "I won't. Papa, it doesn't have to end like this."

Ha.

"But it does, Lira," he said, taking his wet hand over hers, and forcing her to grip the hilt of the knife, "This world is cruel. You need to take life into your hands, damn everyone else. Consequences will plague you," he whimpered. "But do not let that stop you. I am giving you the only thing I have left to give."

"Papa!"

"Kill me Lira!" he squealed. "Unless you do that, you'll never be self-reliant! You must depend on yourself. And no one else. Take your life in your hands, you must know what it's like to take the life of another. Or you'll never grow beyond your own immaturities."

"Papa—"

"Lira!"

"Papa!"

She cried, closing her eyes. Pivoting herself, she thrust the blade into her papa's chest. His heart caved and the life left his eyes as he collapsed onto the floor, gore pouring out in front of it. She felt the heavy weight of what she had done, of what she was compelled to do. She wept with her father's body on the floor, but she knew time was running out. She had to act quickly if his corpse was to be salvageable; after all, she couldn't let the rats get him first.

She tore away his clothes and cut his flesh into pieces, throwing them into a cauldron, heating them. Piece by piece she cooked him, careful to salvage every bit. During one such instant, she heard the scurrying of rats in the corner, and to her dismay, the rats were already trying to eat what was left of her precious father. She gritted her teeth, and stomped over with a ladle, striking the ground with it, scattering the rats into the nearby corner, until they disappeared into the confines of the walls.

She completed the work she set out to do. She took parts of his skeleton and set it up, laying it against the wall. As she packed the meat back up, she thought about what it was she might do next, but first, she must cherish this memory, this dreadful gift that was equally a curse to her own life, and what remained of her sanity. She crawled to papa's carcass and wrapped the bones around her as she sat in his pool of coagulated life essence.

Ha! You should see your face! The look of it just screams terror, but need I remind you—this is life. Everyday life, infested by corrupt morality that only pushes them further into the dark, furthering the blackness of the decaying spirits of their own souls, pushing them further into insanity. Such a dreadful thought, wouldn't you agree, Alkel?

Part Seven

Alkel, I hope you're getting really intimate with that bucket. You need another one? That last bit was kind of disgusting, don't you think? There were so many problems with the world, that being one of them. In my time, we used to think of rites of passage being some form of activity. However, times have changed, and maturity seemed to come with how soon someone kills someone else.

What's that?

Ah, yes, the disastrous sludge of the Abyss, yes, they could have left their hovels, but truth be told Alkel, just like my question before: what are they supposed to eat? Where are they supposed to go? Some people might think that outside the walls might be better, but as I mentioned before, that arena is far worse.

Mother, could you make a hole in the ground for him to dump his vomit? Or provide another bucket? Another bucket it is then. Alkel, here.

Don't be too disheartened, Alkel, for the story takes an uncomfortable turn. Uncomfortable because of that? Oh, no. Dear no. Uncomfortable for how wholesome this seems, at least to someone of my degree of angst, anyway. Such wonderful things happen, and make a change for the better, for how long that will be the case has yet to be seen, but it did get better.

You see, for obvious reasons, Lira couldn't stay there. So, the next morning, she went to Burkam's hovel, early in the morning with the slabs of meat, both from the theft at the marketplace, and then her father. She kept his skull hidden in her sack, and she would cherish it till the end of her days, or at least until the bone decayed. The reality was one wasn't that far from the other. So, she went to his mother's hovel, and presented all the food to her, in exchange for protection. A pseudo adoption, as it were. Another mouth to feed, in exchange for another day where they didn't have to go scrounging for food.

The dung in the corner filled the air, and her only distraction, was the hue of an orange light, a flame lighting up the iron in the house, and the pristine and familiar sound of footsteps down the hall, climbing carefully down the stairs. Lira averted her gaze from the bag of meat and hopped down, the strap around her shoulder swaying with her.

She walked to the doorway and Burkam's mother presented her with a scowl of half broken teeth, licking her lips rather hungrily. She should have had scraps to eat, but perhaps, was Burkam hiding edibles from even his own mother? Eh, he might be nefarious, but even he has his own standards. As long as he didn't cross the line he drew himself, he would be fine. He didn't care about anyone else's line, just his own.

"What ya doin' 'ere?" she said. "He sleepin'. Get home. Git!"

Lira felt a bony hand, a slap across her swollen face. Her face turned and she stifled a yelp for help, ignoring the pain, for her heart was already in so much pain from being alone in this world, this world without hope, and the only commodity more valuable than hope was food and water, of which she now only had one of those things. She gulped and turned back to Burkam's mother.

"I haven't a home to return to," she said, and that stirred something in Burkam's mother as her hand reached into the satchel, feeling the different textures of the various meats inside. The scent from the meat inside offset the stench. She took two pieces out, and Lira noticed the dissimilarity, the one from the exotic meat and the other, flesh cut off from her father. She nibbled one. "You see. There isn't anywhere for me to go."

"What ta stop ya from cuttin' us up?" Burkam's mother pushed her back. "Ye sliced up yer father, who's next?"

If wondering, Alkel, I can't help but think one might have suggested under the notion as to how Burkam's mother came to that conclusion. Lira's father had become a bit of a recluse as of late, but the two did know each other. Trusted one another? Not so much.

"I—" she stammered, trying to come up with some reasonable response in an environment that would be hostile to her. But truth be told, as you can very well realize, the act of her living defiantly, was hostile in itself. "He told me to. I begged him to stop, to not give me the knife, but he persisted, and persisted until I couldn't take it anymore, and I broke. I pushed the knife into his chest, and he begged me to kill him, and cook him. Ye see, there wasn't anything I could do. I didn't have a choice and there was nothing at all anyone could do."

Burkam's mother softened, or rather, her heart softened the stubbornness of her core to some degree. For what purpose, I know not. "I understand," she said, and took the satchel from her. She took a boney hand, and combed her fingers through Lira's hair. Kneeling on the ground, she looked Lira in the eye, and of course, as you might imagine, Lira wasn't sure if she could trust such a kind gesture, for Burkam's mother said, "You may stay here, in Burkam's room, I've only got the two. In return, you'll help Burkam with the housework while I'm gone. Understand?"

"Y—yes," she stammered, crying, and she rolled her fists in her crying eyes.

"Burkam!" his mother called, "Get yer ass down he'e! It is time to break your fast."

Why was she so kind? Burkam's mother? Ha. Alkel, that was not kindness, no, not one bit. You see, it seems we may never get to find out Burkam's mother's motives, for they were never realized. And henceforth, as far as Lira was concerned, they were irrelevant. This wasn't compassion, as it was once seen in my time. Yes, compassion, that is the word for it. I almost lost it there. It's been so many millennia since I've had cause to use said word. I surprise even myself that I remember what it means. Well, Alkel, what you are seeing is nothing than a symbiotic relationship. That is, one receives something in service to some degree for another. Of course, that is just the simplest way I can think to frame it so that you might understand.

Why don't you think of your servants. Steril needs them to do their work, or else things falls apart, and in exchange, he provides for them food and shelter, shitty shelter, I might add, but shelter nonetheless that protects them from the rain. Well, at least most of the time. But perhaps a teaching moment has presented itself to me, and I'll take it upon myself, and use the same scenario. Imagine, that in your experience, you see one of your servants struggling to perform their duties. What do you do? If you had compassion, you'd be compelled to give them a break at the very least or offer to do their tasks for them for the remainder of the day and say nothing.

What was that?

Ah, a question, one too familiar. Why would anyone do anything but to get recognition for it? Truly I say unto you, Alkel, if a man or woman ever did anything just for the recognition, said person is worthless to Mother. Do you find yourself such a person, Alkel? Are you useless? I thought not. You're much too dense to be as nefarious as that. As ignorant as you might be, you're not useless.

Back to Lira, Burkam, and his mother, whose name was not revealed to me. They sat around the table, carefully passing the plate along with the meat she brought as a sort of offering, you understand. Lira took her portion, Burkam his, and his mother hers. The children were formally introduced by his mother, for reasons unknown, as Burkam's new sister, and such a tragic display of affection, in one way or another.

Hmm? Oh, I am not so crude as to suggest that, though, your estimation isn't exactly far from the truth, dare I say.

They ate together, and even shared a few laughs at the table. You might imagine, Lira, a smile cracked upon her lips, blushing in her cheeks before coming back to the sudden realization of the reality that she was eating an unnamed animal and parts of her father. They all were shameless in their reprieve, and yet this is where they are, this is where they all were—in a constant need of others to suffer in their place. But while it might be easy for someone like Burkam, or, in your case, Sar, to murder their individual consciences, it was not so easy for Lira.

Then the rain came again. It was dreadful, they needed water, but not that water, and she, of course, was in torn clothes that needed serious washing, and she herself was long overdue for a bath, a shower, anything of the sort to clean the filth on her skin. But what world is there where water was abundant? It was abundant in my time. Seventy percent, if memory serves right, though less than one percent of that was drinkable, but with certain devices we could make the other sixty-nine percent drinkable. You could dance around in the rain without fear of it burning your skin off. Rarely does that happen in the rain, it's often better to assume the acidity of the rain is hazardous, like it was a few short nights ago.

You could imagine the fear pumping through her heart as her newly adopted mother went to the edge of the doorway leading outside. You could imagine her mother raising her nose up against it, to scoff at its smugness. Sniffing the air, she then saw fit to stretch out her hand, and the rain fell upon it. There was no steam.

"Burkam!" she cried out. "Get the linen. Now! Lira, you help him."

The two children immediately got up from the table, and scurried about for the linen, and the two heaved a large barrel. It was heavy, as that's really all they have for storage, not those horse-hair barrels you keep around. These were metal. The two of them struggled to bring it outside and Lira felt it slice into her hand again. She squinted but she mustn't let her new family down.

She finally made it to the threshold of the door, and she remembered, as you could imagine, the pain, the searing poison cascading on her skin as if she was dumped in a pool of acid. She winced and gasped as she stumbled back onto the floor, and pulled her knees up to her chest as Burkam pulled the linen barrel outside, the rain still pouring as her new mother drew a line across from one lantern to the next. Her mother took the linen and proceeded to wash them in a bucket, hanging them outside as the water berated their nastiness, who knows what sorts of nasty business they were in.

Burkam pushed past her, as she looked curiously outside, but fearful all the same. They were not burning. She caught glimpse of her mother, who scowled, and marched right up to her, gripping firmly her forearm. Lira was terrified, and struggled to get away, but her mother had an iron grip, you understand. Lira was dragged out into the pouring rain. She was surprised, though, having the bout with the acid the previous evening, she was none too keen on bathing in it.

The cold drops of moisture fell upon her face, and it was like a soft hand brushing up against her. She couldn't describe it, but in a gasp as she stood up, weakly, I might add, and her mother looked down on her, squatting, caressing her cheek like a mother would her child, or rather, is supposed to.

"Take your clothes off," her mother said, as she herself started to strip in the rain.

She heard the clamor of buckets coming behind her, and Burkam placed them all on the ground, catching the rain from the air, and the drops of water in a pale echoed like a bell. He too started to strip, and handed his clothes to their mother, who took them and washed them with the water that poured in it and wrung them out. Her mother's hand reached out to her, ready for Lira's clothes. So, without wanting to disappoint further, or incur her wrath, our dear little Lira took her remaining clothes off and handed them to her mother, who washed them and hung them on the line.

Ha. This was almost funny. A nice change in pace, a bit of warmth on the heart after so much tragedy, in so short a time. The three of them held hands with one another, dancing in the rain, allowing it to strike against their skin, the clothes flapping in the wind. Alkel, yes, this does in fact happen, but you must understand, there are only so many rainfalls that can be trusted, and let us not forget, much of these linens are few more than bare threads.

Oh, would you look at that? The door is open. I guess mother is satisfied then, you may leave and delve into whatever it is. Do with your life what you want. Not like there's much left of it.

Oh?

You want to know what happened to Lira? Well, she, Burkam, and their *mother,* live happily ever after. That's a fucking lie. She is alive, don't you worry. But is a life like this truly worth living? Sometimes, Alkel, and for some of us, death is the happiest ending we could hope for. I've been denied that sweet release.

62

Congratulations, you did it, you beautiful reader. It should please you to note that I'm unlikely to try something like this again, and if you made it to the end, you deserve a pat on the back, and you should definitely head over to the retailer, online where you purchased this book from and leave a review, non-spoiler of course, no one likes books to be spoiled, no matter how unorthodox the storytelling is. You know how unusually this type of narrative is, since, odds are, you've not come across a book set up like this. I have other stories in this world to tell, and I'm attaching to this, a never before seen or published one also in this world, a different part of this world, and in a more traditional sense.

This will be featured in an anthology which I will be publishing, likely in 2024. More on this later.

World building can be a challenge, and one which I take head on. As a reader, all writers are readers, we want to get a feel of what the world is like, upon finishing a book. Now, I don't need to tell you why the narrative style is quite restrictive, because the narrator assumes you understand certain details of the world, which of course, you don't. There are also very subtle things of which there is a reason for it but since that detail has very little to do with the story, you are simply forced to ask the question with which there is no way to find the answer. Yet. I will not mention what some of these questions are, and I ask you to discuss them amongst yourselves, but simply ask, this question that I have, is there an answer to it for me? Is this answer here? Or is it forthcoming in subsequent books? There will be other books in this world, and originally I planned an epic, and I'm not entirely sure if I want to commit to that since I've "The Holy Grail War" saga to write, and that will take decades.

I've decided for the time being to write smaller novelettes, short stories, or novels on the short side to tell, that doesn't delve into large tomes. Just trying to make things manageable. With this being said, stay grim my friends, it's a dark world out there, dare we make it grey?

Submissions!

I mentioned before, at the end of this, is a short story, okay, really it's a novelette in the back of this book; I clearly can't follow my own damn instructions. This novelette is the rough draft, so if you want to get a before and after, well, you've got it! This novelette is not yet formerly titled. This novelette will be polished, and edited to no small degree when it is published in the Holy Grail Publishing's first external project: A Grimdark Anthology, titled, "No Happy Endings."

This is for a 2024 Anthology. So, if you come across this notice after it's been published, it's a little late. However, if I thoroughly enjoy this project, keep on the look out because I will likely be doing anthologies more or less frequently.

If you are interested, send a query letter to Holygrailpublishing21@gmail.com. Subject: Grimdark Anthology.

Within the query, tell me about your characters, their stakes, tell me the ending.

Suggestions: This must be grimdark, so violent, dystopian, gritty. Cussing in books I accept quite liberally. This must, generally speaking, be amoral. Hope to read some of your material soon.

More books!

<u>The Holy Grail War: The Hedgehog; The Nihilistic Neverending Nightmare.</u> Available at your favorite Online retailer, or physical bookstore.

~The Gods live among us; in their pursuit of the Holy Grail they are about to turn our world into their battlefield.

Bonus Short Story!

Keneira stared out towards the darkened skies, her sister clasping tightly to her free hand while her spare hand weighed heavily on her opposite side, a chain bound to her wrist, a ball of iron and glass, lights and smoldering embers inside, cackling, providing a light. The cobblestones in front of her was the road onwards towards the hunting grounds, some barrows, and an old cemetery Jera liked to visit, their mother was at rest. It had been three summers since her passing as they walked the bare road. The green orbs up in the sky still illumined, it was safe, for now at least, as she took her first steps forward. They'd be back, just in time for dinner for her father's servants were preparing several boars for the wedding festival.

It was not a wedding she approved of, her little sister, barely past eight summers herself. Wedded to the disgusting Lorshmo, son of Crushma, Prince of the North. Rumor had it the King himself went a little impotent, and the poor son, the bastard, found early this morning balls deep in a damned hog, as if her father's brothels, of which was offered last night, was subsequently refused for the sake of purity. Dreadfully so, she must admit, this was her own fault for marrying a low-born, but she loved him, and wouldn't divorce him to save her sister. Oh Gods. To even think to have the same prick that defiled some hog inside her was disgusting, she nearly vomited at the thought.

"I want to see mummy," Jera said, her hand squeezing her own, gently, as she could. "Come, take me to mummy."

"But of course," Keneira smiled, looking at her sister with the flame lighting her face. The hair was tied into a nice little bun, the clothes were mournful, to say the least, and with a weakness about her shoulders, her hand tucked a few strands of hair behind her ears. "Just let me take care of the light."

She twisted the iron clasp at the top, opening a port with the glass, and embers danced inside the cage, emitting a little more illuminations. No telling really how much longer those orbs would stay lit, and when they did, the Abyss would encroach upon them, and this lantern would be the only thing either of them had to shield them from the dark, and the monsters that dwelt within them. Yes, yes, the cemetery too was part of the Abyss, but with this lantern, they could traverse it safely, as safe as one ever dared. Tightening her grip on her sister's hand, they stepped forward, the metal cage creaked with each step.

"Keneira," Jera spoke in her high-pitched voice. "What was it like?"

"What was what like?" She asked, observing the road, seeing the break in the path rising upwards, soil, there was, and dying plants. *She is far too young for this.*

"Marriage," she said. "What's it like?"

"Did father never tell you?" she replied, leading her sister up the path ascending. She turned her head to look down at her sister, her brown braid brushed to the side of her shoulder covered in a green tunic. The eyes were innocent, gaping as if she herself was crying, not ready to face her future, not ready to continue on with tradition. No, her father already had one child who broke tradition, he needn't another.

"No," she answered, and Keneira knew, her father too was bastard enough to give her the responsibility for explaining these sensitive things. The bastard!

"It is a wonderful thing," she replied. "Not without it's difficulties, certainly," her eyes gazed up to the sky. The air seemed lighter. "Come, let us not tarry for long. Remember, stay in the light."

"What's in the dark?" Her sister asked. Too young, and too sheltered was she from the dark that such tragedies went amiss. Sometimes it was so easy to forget she simply didn't know.

"Monsters," she sighed, stepping upwards, taking her sister with her. "Careful, and quiet steps must we take."

They stepped forward, the path of the soil was soft, easier on their feet. The light from the green orbs faded as they drew further away from the path, the light from the lantern swayed, and the Abyss, like black smoke swirled around them, trying to penetrate the perimeter of light it created, but to no avail. Funny thing, really, darkness cannot survive in the light, but this world had so little of it. The path brought them to a plateau, and the light shone several stones, metal rods stuck into the ground, bones, and makeshift plants and gifts from those whose dead were buried here. Save for one, and she walked Jera to it, the stone, a large one, a slate like a book. Upon it was inscribed the details of her mother, really, just her name: Mira, Countess of Morin, wife of Kira, mother of Keneira and Jera.

And underneath that was written: May the traditions protect you.

"Here she is, but be careful," she spoke solemnly, the lantern rested on the ground as she knelt, hands clasped over one another. She silently prayed a prayer, but to which God, she knew not anymore. How could ay God have wanted to creature such a dark, pitiful place? None. For better, for worse, good or evil, this world benefited no one, save for perhaps some sadistic lunatic.

"Flowers!" Jera shrieked. "Keneira, we forgot to bring flowers!"

"Oh my," Keneira turned to her. "You might be right. Go and grab some by the garden over there."

"Nothing e'er grows there!" she whined, fists at her side.

"Yes, but still, why don't you look. Or take a flower from one of the other graves. Those still work too, just stay I the light." Keneira heard the steps scurry off as she continued to look at her mother's tombstone. Squatting down, her hand reached out to touch the stone, remembering what her mother looked like before she passed. A tear rolled down her cheek, bowing her head. "I love you." She wept with the coming of the passing of time. "I can't. I just can't. Baudet is here, but he is not you, and Jera, she looks so much like you, mother, it hurts to look at her sometimes."

"Keneira!" her sister shrieked.

She turned her head. The braid whipped past her. Eyes darting her vision towards the garden, a pitiful display of a flowerbed, there was nothing save the black canvas behind it. *Damnit.* She stood grabbed the lantern, her blood pumped through her veins with each step, the light surrounding her in this cemetery, and she traversed the darkness of the Abyss, the light penetrating its hide, and the swirls of black smoke pushed back with the strength of the embers flaring from within their chamber.

Braving the dark, she felt the sludge creep into her boot, grimacing, heart pounded as the cold of the Abyss caressed her as she passed through the unknown. Mist, did she exhale from her lips as she pushed through the sludge, following her sister's voice. "Jera!" she cried, the weight of the sludge weighing down on her. Each step was heavy, like a ball and chain was tied to her feet, shackling her oppressively. Peering past her vision swept, as the dark touched the orb of light around her, she feared the worst, and then, a squeak, heard she in the middle of it, a ruckus of tumbling rocks striking the ground.

"Keneira!" the voice shrieked again. "Keneira!"

"Jera!" She called, a rasp in her voice, and she sprinted towards it, the swiveling lantern squeaked with thee sudden jerk in the force she swung, and found her sister, the brave poor fool, dash at her from the dark. "Jera!" she snapped, kneeling down, hands on her arms, nervously looking for markings of anything, bites, bleeding, nothing. "What did I say?"

"But I smell—"

"It doesn't matter, you don't brave the Abyss!"

"Why!" Jera exclaimed. "You do it all the time!"

To get away from father. To get away from—what am I running from? She gasped, and that was all she could say. "It's dangerous. You don't know what's out there, and the Abyss can claim you." She reached forth, embracing her sister. "I'm sorry, I was scared. I didn't mean to frighten you."

"But Keneira," her sister spoke into her ear. "Come with me,"

"We really should be getting back now, did you find the flower for Mother's grave?" she asked, standing, her eyes locked with her sisters innocent gaze.

"I found lots and lots and lots of things," she said, a sneer curled upon her lips. Had it come from anyone else's mouth, she'd think she was up to something. "Come and see, you'll like them."

"Very well, but we mustn't say for much longer. Hold my hand, and remember, stay in the light!"

"Yeah, yeah," her sister brushed off the comment, taking her hand and she pulled her.

Keneira let her little sister lead fer for a moment, the sludge still heavy, and the air grew thicker, and warmer for some reason she simply couldn't reconcile. The light illumined the dark until they got to the mouth of a cave, stalagmites, and stalactites formed into a large ravenous mouth, and there seemed to be something fuzzy growing on the stoney teeth. Her heart raced as her sister brought her closer to the cave. She couldn't have a nefarious mind. . .could she? Perish the thought, but onward she went, and the air grew warmer. Walking further into the mouth of the cave; there was a large open space in the center, where it was clear, streams of water. . . in abundance?

With reckless abandon, she darted forward to the water, and her sister followed. The giggles echoed off the walls as they came to the stream. The metal lantern creaked, the light still shining through its glass. At the stream, she knelt down, cupped her hand, and placed it in the cool water, brought it to her lips,

and the refreshing liquid poured down her gullet. Exhaling a sigh of refreshment, she looked up, her sister walking through the stream into a clearing, and there was an artifact, of some sort. A brown pole, thicker than a house, and vein-like shapes of itself crawled to the streams where the tips rested, digging themselves into the earth. Large things like those on the ground scraped the roof of the cave, some thick, some thin, all with green oval shaped bracts. Rustling, as they lay above her, and some arms stretched down, hovering over another pedestal.
She walked towards it with here sister, hating herself for trusting something like this so easily, but she was drawn to the artifact.

One of these arms stretched forward, branching out even, like little firm hands. The light from the lantern lit up an orb on which it lay, a red orb, with another brown stick at thee top of it, and another bract. She took her hand, covered it, brought it to her face, flicking it's firmness. Raising it to her nose, she sniffed it, but nothing caught her attention, and she opened her mouth, took a bite from it. Crunchy, hard, and. . .sweet.
Moisture it was inside, the white pale flesh. She took hers to her sister. "Here, try it, it's tasty!"

Her sister took it in her hands, and immediately, Keneira wanted it back. She didn't know what t was, but it was delicious, more delicious than all the other dried fruit, meat, and various breads she ate every day. Even living underneath the safety net of being te heir of the Countess' seat, there were subjects and limitations as to what was available. Her sister took her hand, bit into the apple, a bright blush filled her cheeks, smiling, she chewed the fruit, whatever it was, and walked towards the other side of this cavernous opening, and little flower bed, only, these flowers were vibrant, healthy, not grey or black like those above.

Her sister was enthralled by one such flower and took it in her hands. The pedals were bright yellow, a large red center, a thick green stem. Her sister discarded the fruit, and it rolled towards the stream. She resented giving it to her, but her sister was precious, even if she didn't share the rest of it with her. She'd never taste it again. . .but perhaps, she knew where this was now, she could come back? Yes, it wasn't a complete total waste. A flower, the golden petals, were plucked from the garden, and she came to her sister, reaching up. "It's beautiful," she said, reaching up and tucked it behind her ear. "Like you."

"Well, aren't you thee sweetest thing," she fastened the flower behind her ear. "Did you find one acceptable for mother?"

Jeanette looked at the garden again, plucked a purple flower, and presented it to her. "This one, it was the color of her eyes."

"Yes," Keneira smiled. "That will do just fine."

They left the cave, but upon approaching the cemetery, Keneira looked back to where the cave was, the darkness swirled around it. Such a place, where the world was left with lacking, with water in short supply, plants were dying, or lived rather shortened lives, in that cave, it was abundant. She might come back here, to get some water. It wasn't terribly far from their land. She looked up in the sky, in the distance, the faint green hue was beginning to fade.

"Jera," she knelt down. "We must be quick, it's late. This flame can protect us only so much."

"Very well," Jera spoke sharply, scurrying towards the grave site, tucked the flower by the stone atop which their mother lay, and she retreated back to her side, ready to go.

Mother, I love you.

Keneira returned Jera to the fief. The land was lit up by torches of burnable metal that doesn't consume, and other miscellaneous materials. Dogs and cats roamed with their owners keeping steady watch. A bonfire, cackling, roasting the smell of a boar. Still cooking, for the feast later, prepping for tomorrow's wedding. She still had hesitancies about that. As she walked with Jera, her sister turned to her, and said, "Can I go play?"

"Of course," she smiled. "Just stay within the guard's sight, will you? And stay in the light!" She couldn't risk her thinking she could go into the Abyss without any form of light. The Abyss, she didn't know all that was in it, except uncharted territory.

"Ken!" A hard, thick voice called out. She swiveled, and beheld a man in his thirties, strong like an ox he was. "Where ye off to?"

"I was going to get change 'fore the—"

"Stop it with that, plenty enough time later," Jorgan spoke harshly. "Can't let ye a'm rust up now can we?"

"Here? You want me to duel here? Now!" There were lots of people here, and she didn't want people knowin' her stance was still weak when wielding her sword. A little kick to the thigh would send her tumbling down.

"Just 'round the road," he spoke, and he led her away from all the people. "You carried yer sword with ye, did ye not?"

"Did ye bothe' ta look?" she said, her hand on the pommel of her blade. She wished she'd the time to set her crossbow down somewhere, it was heavy with the iron block attached to it. Sturdy thing, that."

"Yes, well, as heir to the Countess' seat, you must be prepared, and disciplined," he said to her as they were well away from everyone's sight. "Didn't want to publicly disgrace ye, now, we best start workin' ono that stance now."

He was right, even a countess was destined to fight should the occasion called for it, and there was no shortage of callings for occasions with the Eastern nation, the brutish Nezkamas threating discourse on their flank. The men to the south rarely came to their aid, that was to say, never would they come for their aid unless they could raid and pillage, and rape their women for hazard pay. Griping, she stood, draw here sword, two hands on her pommel as she held it out, ready. Her back leg bent, ready to pivot, but her front leg, still twisted at the ankle, more than half her body weight leaned on the hind.

"Steady that stance!" he said pointed. "Hold hat blade tightly. Tighter! I said!"

"This is my tightest grip, ye bastard!" she swore.

"Ha!" he swung his sword at her. Tilting her body, she parried the blade, but the force of the strike pushed her. "If that is the tightest grip ye can muster, I'd hate to see the sorry fate your house will have. After all, yer the only one who can wield a sword. Poor little Jera is far too young."

"Too young! Poor baby girl," she said, swiveling her feet and she threw her sword at him, attempting to nick his finger, he retracted his strike, and kicked the end of her sword. "Who will ever come for her aid."

"Well," he thrust his sword at her, completely exposed, it grazed here neck. She ducked down, twisted her body and danced on her feet away from his reach. "Not that you'll have to worry about that much, tradition and all."

"She's too young, Jorgan," she spoke. "Far too young to be given in marriage."

"Yes," he scratched his head, sheathing his sword. She did so in kind. "ot much we can do about that."

"Why not?" she asked. "My father is the head count—"

"Head count or not, doesn't matter, whatever the king says, does," he snapped. "Keneira, you must discard your own found morality, you might learn something. There is no right, no wrong, there is just what is."

"And for you, what is, just is?" she asked. This was a rather short sparing match, did her swords play partner decide it was time for a good lecturing?

"Just. Just is. Justice," he grunted. "Traditions were set in stone, and they ought not be uprooted like pointless weeds. Keneira, you know, you know too well that my fate is tied to the house. The house survives, so do I. Justice," he growled. "Is just a mere word. There is nothing just in this world in which we live. Get used to it."

"What!" she exclaimed. "But what are our traditions that we s—"

"Your mother believed in our traditions, our customs," he said. "Who are you to deny them? We don't get to decide what they are. Trust me when I say—"

"No, Jorgan!" she snapped. "What are traditions but man-made constructs!"

"And what are you going to do?" he asked. It was more a statement than a question. One of several in which he had asked in the future, to stop her passion, to force a moment of logic within her. It worked every time. What would she do? Nothing. That's what. She'd see her little sister off, married to that pig pookin' bastard! Removed from their house, inherited the Kingship, while she would be left with the countship of his fief, with her lowborn husband. There was nothing she could do, or else, risk the wrath of the king, face his justice by way of public hanging, and the spectators would dance seeing her body swinging with creaking rope, gasping for breath.

"I don't know," she finally stammered.

"Good," he said. "Then nothing is what you should do. As young as she is," he finally sighed, taking a seat upon a rock. "Young as she is, it would be most unwise to deny the will of the King. The Prince, less than reasonable."

"I understand," she said.

"Good, see to it you do," he replied, standing and proceeded to walk towards one path leading to the butchery. "

The Iron walls echoed with the various footsteps into her ears. Golden hue of flamelight from candles layered across the grand hall. Loud conversations to be had on all corners of the room. Food, there was, aplenty, for the King provided for the feast, and her father, Kira, provided thee venue, the servants to which would cook and prepare the food. The music played with leather instruments, strings from horse hair.

Keneira ate from here plate, a turkey leg, roasted in front of her as she looked from across the hall. Her father and King Crushma spoke to one another, laughing like long friends, but she knew, the purpose of such niceties was always political. The only thing she could understand was the laughter, and to their side, the future betrothed, Lorshma and Jera sitting at the King's right hand side. The dreadful prince was already intertwining his filthy little fingers in her hair, laughing as his future bride looked away, trying to keep herself busy, occupied and distracted with the plate of grey lettuce on her plate.

"Try not to think on it too much," Baudet said at her side, reaching in, pecking her on the cheek. He scraped thee plate with his eating utensils.

"Dravel, dravel, dravel!" she growled. "Dare I say you don't understand," and why would he? He wasn't high born like her. Perhaps she did in fact marry poorly. No. Objectively speaking, she did, all in the sake of love, for love's sake. Perhaps her decision to throw tradition in the dung heap led to here sister slowly being groomed to mate with whatever that *thing* was. Only a *thing* would dare pook a pig. "You wouldn't understand. Leave it alone."

"I can't leave it alone," he said, turning to her, brushing a strand of hair behind her ear. "You'll take it out on me later."

"When have I ever taken out my problems on you," she said. "I love you. You know that."

"As do I, and I know you love me," his hand touched her chin, tilting her gaze up. "But you do it every day. Perhaps you conveniently forget I'm lowborn, a stable boy, that's all I ever was, but when I caught such infatuation from you, I couldn't help but pursue you." He gulped down the rest of his ale. "Speaking of which, I've horses to feed now. Try not to do anything rash will you?"

She shook her head, kissing him firmly on the lips as he left. The chair moved, and he disappeared behind the plains of people, and in the center of the room, people started to dance. Perhaps when she was countess, she could enjoy a dance with the stable boy, her husband. Lorshmo took her sister's hand and out on the dance floor. Of course, with the promise of tomorrow, Jera couldn't very well deny such a gesture for more reasons than one. He stroke her hair, the one she braided, and who knew if the dirty little bastard at least brushed his hands through some water first before touching her. Gritting her teeth, she took a draught of ale.

"Poor dear, your husband seemed to abandon you before the dance," a voice called, and she turned. A strong red-headed woman looked at her with a lovely dress. "Dare I keep you company? Or will you push me away?"

"By all means, Count Mala," she motioned to the empty seat behind her. "Take your seat, it has now become available."

"I see," Mala elegantly took her seat next to her. "Dreadfully, I must say, a girl as young as yourself should be out dancing. Such a shame he left."

"Well, he is a stableboy," she said. "Father doesn't approve of him."

"No," Mala replied, taking a sip of her ale which, she brought with her. "No doubt. A little strong about the shoulders, you know how to choose the right stock."

"We're not livestock, Mala," she snapped. "Treat my husband with some dignity. He gets enough of that from him, he doesn't need it from you."

"Sorry to suggest that," Mala apologized. "Milady."

"Nothing to forgive," she permitted herself to smile as she turned her gaze back to her sister, and emotions betrayed her of the disgust she had for the King. She felt her teeth gritting.

"Milady," Mala said, her hand stretching forward, clasping atop hers with an iron grip. "Might I have your ear a moment?"

"Yes, Count Mala," she turned over to her, putting her hand atop Mala's. She had to admit, the countess' grip was tighter than she expected. "What pray tell, reason do you have to infect mine ear with your words?"

"Oh, what's court life without a little friendly gossip," she sneered, bending forward. "You see, I have it quite on good authority, dear, that you do not approve of this marriage."

"No," she replied, turning her gaze from her. "But that's hardly a surprise, I am quite vocal on this matter."

"Except now," Mala replied. "Think not that I wasn't listening to your minute quarrel with your beloved."

"She's too young, Mala," she said. "Too young."

"She's too young, he's not that old, perhaps just a few years older than you," she said. "Marrying young, especially for such political gain, your father is no fool, is not out of our customs."

"To hell with our customs!" She whispered sharply. "To hell with them all."

"To that," Mala drank. "You and I are in quite the agreement. Such drivel. What those of the lesser stock than you and I fail to understand, is if you understand customs and traditions, you can make them say whatever it is you want them to say. Things change, so do our twists on the old lore goes, to fit our needs. I didn't rise to my station by merely following tradition. Now, look at me, a Count, not a mere countess. When you come into the seat when your father dies, you can make it that your stableboy is the countess, and you the Count."

"And what did you do to make yourself the Count?" Keneira took the ale to her lips, poised to take a sip. "Surely there was a more complicated solution to your individual disposition."

"I killed him," she answered with a smile as ale slipped down her lips. She coughed. "The count, that is. After a night of passionate love making, I poisoned his morning ale. It was beautiful."

"The Four Gods," she wiped the ale and spit from her chin with a cloth. "You're bold to admit that before me. What's to say I don't—"

"Hush now," Mala replied, two fingers pressed to her lips. "We could all stand a little more violence."

"Are you suggesting I kill my father?" she whispered. "I'll not—"

"No," Mala cackled. "That would accomplish nothing. You'd become the Count, of course, but it would still be expected to join the two houses, and Jera would still be wedded to the beastial prince tomorrow evening, and then, pair it with a lovely funeral. And where would you be? Count, sure, but alas, the whole point of becoming Count would be nigh useless to you."

Keneira coughed.

"Though," Mala took another drink. "If something were to happen to the King and Prince tomorrow, I might be inclined to ignore it. Let it be known," Mala winked as she stood from her seat. "I'm not suggesting you to do anything. After all, accidents do happen.

Keneira yawned as she walked her sister up the iron stairs through their home. It was a large home, some candles, torches, paintings on the walls were lit up in the lateness of the hour. Looking to here sister, she noted the little girl was rubbing her eyes with her dress, a few stains through messy eating. Keneira, as she walked her sister to her bedroom to tuck her in for the night of such an abomination, here mind was infiltrated again by thee words, harsh, though they were, and yet, a certain subtlety about Count Mala, presenting her with a solution, though, not explicitly suggested. Accidents happened, and of course, the killing of Mala's own husband was suggestive enough. Despite the abomination, she doubted she could do go through such a solution.

Arriving at the door, she opened it, creaking it did, the iron as it swung on its hinges, berating the wall behind it. She led her tired sister to her bed, yawning. "I'm not tired," she protested as the door slammed shut behind them.

"Come here," Keneira giggled, taking her hand and leading her to the bed. "Come, let's get you changed. You've a big day tomorrow. You'll need to be rested well enough."

"I don't like him," Jera growled. "I don't. Why do I have to?"

"Tradition and politics," Keneira sighed, kneeling down. Brushing with a finger a tear from her sister's eye.

"But I don't want to, I don't like him, there's just, they will take me from mummy!" she cried. Yes, that was a certainty, for with her, her mother couldn't go, not while her corpse lay inn a hole in the ground. "Can you talk to daddy? Make him change his mind?"

"Hey, hey, hey," she stifled a tear, kept it in the lid so her sister couldn't see the turmoil in her own heart, the cruelty of this barbaric world where people, no matter how high a station they held, were subject to be traded like livestock. "Listen, let's get you to bed. We'll talk more tomorrow."

"But Keneira!" her sister protested, too much. "I don't want to do this!" She cried, kneeling down. Keneira embraced the hug, permitting her sister to cry in her arms. "I don't want to. I don't want to. Let's leave." *And where would we go?*

"I don't know what, or how, but I will do what's good for you," she replied. "Whatever that looks like. Now, Jera, off to bed now. You've a busy day tomorrow."

"What will you do?" her sister changed into a night gown and crawled in her bed.

"I don't know," she said. "Hush now, let me think on it." There just wasn't enough time. Tomorrow will be too busy to think.

"Will you hum for me then, to sleep?" Jera asked. "One last time."

"Of course, my dear little princess,"

She smiled gravely, and tucked her sister in, stroking her braids. She hummed a tune to her. A made-up tune, for she wasn't musical, but that bothered her sister none. The little ears complained little when something was out of tune, and had not yet completely appreciated the talent others had for music, or perhaps, because this tune came from her own voice, her own beat, that it was tolerable. No. That wasn't it at all. It was because it came from her, that despite it's musical flaws, she loved it, and thus fell asleep swiftly.

"Sleep well," she whispered, her hand touched her sister's shoulder. Watching her sleep, she didn't dare leave the bed, for she knew not without any levelof certainty, if she or here sister would sleep peacefully after tomorrow. This may be the last time she could look at her like this, and so, she could permit herself to abandon her husband in bed tonight, he might not understand, but he'll have to accept his lot in life, whatever the future would look like. But for Keneira crawled into her sister's bed, and cuddled beside her, arms wrapped around. He warmth was comforting, if, nothing else was in this world. With little hesitation, her eyelids drew themselves closed, and alas, she knew nothing but the solace. As much as she could tell, there was little else she could manage, and knew not how long this peace would last.

She looked at her sister the following night, before the ceremony. Dreadfully, she'd not thought of a lasting solution to her predicament, but gazing at her sister, her beautiful, subtle gown she held, ringlets of gold set upon her hair, pulled back and braided like she too had a crown upon her head already. Worthy was her sister, of the grandest of crowns. But not like this, not like the drivel that would be placed on her this evening, not like the drivel of a man, dung heaped, again, balls deep into one of her father's horses! That disgusting little wretch! *My sister!*

Jera seemed none too happy either, for why would she be? Not only was the wedding going to take place now, as she was walked into a room with which she would come out and walk down the aisle of the Temple of the Four Gods, but also, her sister had simply failed, or, Keneira guessed, thought her sister just simply did nothing for the sake of tradition. When she became Count, she would do away with all of it, consequences be damned, and whoever has to suffer will, as she had despaired.

"But—"

"You will go through with it," Keneira snapped and relented. "I'm sorry. 'm so sorry. There isn't anything I could do!"

"Very well," her sister sighed, looking down, and then, her eyelids fluttered. Onward then, a pathway to misery.

The door opened, and Keneira took her sisters hand, walking down out, crossing the threshold into the temple. The chairs were seated, a fire over yonder towards thee altar of the four gods, humanoids, they all were, save for two, of which were fashioned from the dreaded Nezka race, the purple bastards. Everyone stood as the music played, and her sister took her first steps, walking rhythmically as she could, towards the dreadfully dressed king-to-be. The sniveling bastard wiped his nose with his sleeve, sick, no doubt, probably going to die by way of venereal disease. *You best not touch my sister with your nasty little prick!*

Mala was dressed in a beautiful gown, her ceremonial sword at her hip. A smile on her face as she traded words silently with one of her body guards. Not too far from her, closer towards the altar of the Four Gods, was Jorgan, dressed in a leather cuirass, but designed for ceremony, he was after all, expecting trouble, and so was the case with such royal weddings, one could never be too careful. The king, and her father were towards the center, looking onward. Keneira refused to scowl as other lesser men ogled their eyes at her sister, walking.

At last, the moment which she thought would never come, and she let her sister go, and joined the prince, the two held hands. Keneira no longer could tell the expression her sister had, but she imagined it was none too pleasant, least of all, the prince, eyes gleamed with excitement, orbs watered as they dd. The man behind him, she knew not his name, but that of the sats of such a man was merely to be the best friend of the groom, no doubt, would try to turn her husband into a cuckhold, but she'd not have it. No, should the bastard try, he'll have two less fruits.

She stared angrily at the Prince, smiling as he was for a conquest he didn't deserve, was far too distracted to see her glaring at him. The friend however, seemed to finally avert his gaze from hers, and she looked at him like this throughout the entire ceremony, this angry, foul tradition. She would burn this temple to the ground. For the sake of tradition, and soon, ah! The sacrifice to cement the marriage. A boar was walked over here by the farmer which raised it and brought it to the priest who was about the say the sacrificial rites and raised his hand with a knife to slay the boar.

"Father, if I may," Keneira said. Was she really considering this? Her gaze shifted to behind the sanctuary, there was a door here, and it led outside. Did she really have it in her? "I'd like to slay it."

"It is strictly forbidden for those of the flock to offer sacrifices to the Four Gods," he turned to her, mouth gaped open like she'd gone mad. But she had in fact gone quite mad.

"Yes," she admitted, a sneer crept upon her lips as the Prince turned to the King. "It isn't exactly illegal now is it? Give me the knife," seeing the priest didn't comply, she turned to her father. "Father, may I slay the boar?"

"Doesn't matter who slays it," the king smiled, superseding the request for aid from her father. "Go on, give her the knife. We're to be one house after all."

"King Crushma," she smiled as she walked towards the priest.

The priest reluctantly handed her the handle of the knife. Gripping it firmly, she bowed too the priest, a smile creeping on her lips. She was going to do it. Her hand pet the boar, which groaned in reply to her touch, and the knife, ceremonial, handle firm within her grasp, caressed the cheek, the cold iron forced it to jerk away, but her hand reached forth, pulling upon its collar. "There, there, it's going to be alright." With uncertainty, she wasn't sure exactly whose nerves she intended to be calming. She took a large breath, the smokey air filled her lungs.

"You bastard!" she turned immediately, stabbing Lorshmo in the face. Retracting her knife, the corpse fell to the floor, not a sound as blood smeared across his face. Before his friend could do anything, she sliced his neck, and with a bloody hand, ignoring all the screams, she took her sister's hand in her own. "We're getting out of here!" But where were they to go?

Here sister squealed at the blood, some sprayed upon her face as she stumbled towards here sister. The priest didn't have enough time to respond, no one did, save for the screaming, confusion of creaking chairs scratching across the floor, and the boar, still growled, for it lived to see another day, or perhaps after tonight, someone would enjoy a bountiful meal.

Disappearing behind the alter, Keneira knew she'd be hunted. She needed her sword! And so first, despite her husband being caught in the middle of the madness, there, he would remain a stableboy, and it would be like the marriage never happened.

"Lorshmo! My Son!" Crushma cried, running over to his son's fallen corpse. "Get her! Get her immediately. Kill her!"

He pulled up his son from the ground, nearly unrecognizable, wiping the blood from his son's face, his beloved child, his only one, lay dead with a slit into his face, bones cracked underneath that dreadful bitch's knife. Kira, he would pay for this. He will fucking hang! Gritting his teeth, he looked at the count, of which, undoubtedly, wanted this. He put Keneira up to the murder of his son who had done nothing wrong. "Bring me his head!"

"Sire," Kira spoke gently. "It grieves me, truly, it does. I did not tell her to do this."

"And yet you respond as if knowing my thoughts," Crushma spoke.

"It's impossible not to know, my Lord," Kira replied. "Jorgan, go fetch them. Bring Jera back to us alive. If it is impossible, then kill Keneira. She is no daughter of mine."

"Don't you dare, he'll help her escape!" Crusha protested. "Mala!"

He looked at the other Count who could be bothered to show up to this wedding. "Seize him!"

"That won't be necessary," Jorgan replied, hand on his pommel.

"Necessary my arse!" Crushma swore. "Curse this house. Curse all of it. We all know you mentored the girl inn sword play. You can't be trusted."

"My loyalty has never been up to debate," Jorgan replied. "Trust me when I say it belongs to this house, and this house alone. Kira has already declared that Keneira belongs not to this house anymore. I will kill her and bring back Jera."

"But you cannot bring back my son," Crushma wept. "Go. Someone hang Kira!"

"And then the house will die!" Jorgan said. "He is the Count!"

"I don't think that's necessary," Mala spoke, Crushma watched her whispering something with one of her messengers. "I think we can hold off on any executions for the treasonous bitch. But, Nezkama are coming. They appeared to have broken off the rest of the flank and are making their way here. Seems they really wanted a red wedding," she laughed. "Well, they got one!"

"Fine," Crushma agreed.

There was a ruckus in the crowd of people, still too shocked to move to permit them to process anything other than the two bodies on the floor, murdered in cold blood, but there was one person who was moving outside his own agency. A man, it seemed, trying to escape, and the King's hand raised up. "Seize that man immediately!" Men and women clad in armor immediately seized him, and he was not one for struggling, and was escorted to the king. He recognized the stableboy; this was the man with whom Keneira shared the cup.

"Where will your wife go?" Crushma asked. He turned to the messenger. "See too it word gets out, a kinig's gold reward will go to the man who brings me her head."

"My Lord," Mala snapped. "You clearly are out of touch with the Count's subjects. They don't want money, it's useless. All that will do is provide reason for others to come and steal from them. Offer them a seat at your table for food; indefinitely."

"No," he said. "Another mouth too feed—"

"Well, you've a Prince no more, so think you can well afford it," Mala suggested.

Crushma gritted his teeth, this Count wasn't exactly replaceable, and she knew it. A bastard of a combination to have amongst the ranks, someone worth more than their weight in gold and untold riches, and likely, knew their precise worth. Shit circumstances all there was, but he could deal with it later, he always did. But now, to this man. "Answer me!"

Grieved as everyone was, soldiers from among the ranks started to depart by way of orders from their captains, to prepare the way for despair, and the violence which would ensue shortly. Why, why can't he get a minute to grieve? Damn Nezkama bastards!

"No!" Baudet said, that was his name, he remembered. "No."

"A man has his price," Mala said, tilting Keneira's husbands face to her, a gleam in her eye. "What's yours?"

Keneira escaped with here sister towards the armor that was much further down. She had not the time to get her own sword, but a practice blade would do, it would fit for their purposes. Running, panting, sweating, her little sister too, hands on her thighs as she bent over, breathing heavily. Thanks the Four Gods they don't dress up so fabulously as the dastardly women in the South do. Dreadful, she found a sword, tied it to her waist, and just encase, scouring over the weaponry with the smith and foundries unattended, she found a crossbow and some bolts, heavy, still. A good solid one-hundred-fifty pounds.

She took her sister's hands in her own. "We're getting you out of here." *South? Yes, we'll be safe there.* "Look," she said to her. "I know it's hard, but we have to keep running. We'll go down to places they cannot or will not follow."

"Mummy," she whined. Of course, she'd be sad about it, the one such course of her actions, the consequences which would no doubt arise with the risks of futility. What other consequences await her tonight? After all, she did not once think this through. "Mummy!"

"Jera," Keneira put her hand on her sister's shoulders. "You were going to be separated regardless, I wish things could be different. I'm saving you?" was she? Or was this something she was trying to convince herself? "I have a friend down in the village. We can stay with him for a time being. Let us go now, we can take a moment, think before they come looking for us."

Exactly how much time had passed? It certainly hadn't been a full day, and yet, a spirit of sleep was coming upon her. She knew she had to be awake, for she knew not she was going to do what she ultimately did, and let alone, for how much longer she'd have to force herself awake.

"Very well," her sister wiped her tears. "Thank you."

"Thank me not yet," she said. *What else am I going to lose tonight?* By the Four Gods, she did not think this through.

Dreadfully aware was she of the discourse throughout the village, people scampering about, wheels carting as if there was nothing to see here. Horses roamed, pulling the carts along. Some people rested, stayed inside their own little homes of iron walls, and some candles lit here, some torches here. She needed a torch, where to find one? No telling really, when she might need to traverse the Abyss, that was actually almost an inevitable fate, for there was not enough light in the night to go around to traverse the roads. Was she mad?

Coming to the door of Mirkur, her sister tugged on her hand firmly. Keneira sighed, squatting with her free hand touching the door. "Jera, it's alright. I know you don't know him, but he's a good person. We can trust him, if, no one else." Her sister nodded, grunting with the pain in her thigh, no less. She noticed it on the sprint to the armory she forced her to undertake. They had no choice really. Keneira nodded, showing her sister she understood her pain, standing up, she knocked on the iron door.

Footsteps echoed from behind it, a light illumined from the crack underneath the door. At last, it pulled open, a man with an thin face, a weak smile, and above all, rags that smelled with flies buzzing around him. Father, another companion of whom he simply would not approve. His smile was brighter, seeing who it was, and with nervousness besides, his eye seemed to be looking at something past her. "Keneira," he said. "Lovely to see you again, it's been an age, since you've been married I think."

"Aye, Mirkur, I agree, it's been too long," she said. "May we come in; this is my sister."

"Of course," he spoke sharply. "Hurry."

She walked in with her sister, permitted Mirkur to shut the door quietly as to not arouse suspicion. She led her sister to the table, chairs, and hoisted her up to the stool so she could sit relatively comfortably. She took a deep breath, and permitted herself a moment to think as Mirkur walked over, sitting across. "What's your name?" he asked.

"It's—it's—" she began to say.

"It's alright," Keneira leaned in close to her sister. "It's alright, you can tell him."

"Juh—Jera," she stammered.

"Lovely name," he smiled. "Trusty, based on the attire, you look like you came from a wedding. Yours?" "A—

aye—" she replied.

"Look," Keneira spoke. "I need help. We need your help."

"Well, by the looks of it, you murdered the groom," he pointed at the blood on her sisters face. "Now, I may not be a smart man, but I recognize blood when I see it. Please tell me who it was?"

"You didn't know?"

"Four Gods," he said. "The Prince. You didn't kill the Prince. Tell me Keneira! Did you, or did you not kill the Prince?"

She heard scattering footsteps from above the ceiling. "Yes," she admitted. "A foul man, if ever there was one."

"We're all foul," he said with a fading smile. "You need to leave. I thought you'd be in trouble, but I didn't think this. Your being here puts my family at risk. I'd do many things for you, Keneira, but not this. Leave, immediately! I'll speak of your presence to know one. Get out. The back door you can use, now leave before—"

"Keneira!" a voice called from the other side. Shit. "We've come for Keneira, come out now. We know she's in there!"

Mirkur stood from the table, walked briskly to the counter. Drawer was pulled out, and a kitchen knife he grabbed. Turning to her, the knife behind his back, he opened his mouth. "Out the back! Now. You brought them here!" Terror seized his face. "You must leave!" He turned to go to the door as she helped her sister from the stool. Fear gripping her, biting a lip until red blood dripped out from her mouth.

"Come," she said, quietly walking towards the back of the house.

"She's not here," Mirkur said, lying to himself, he must have, otherwise, he'd have let them in. "Gt yer own food. I've not enough to spare. You know that."

"I don't want yer food, open the damned door peasant bastard!"

"That's just ru—"

The door swung open, punching him in the face. Mirkur dropped to the ground, the knife behind his back flew out, spinning on the floor. Keneira looked away as she hurried to the window, footsteps echoing faster behind here. "Keneira! Get over here. Get back here!" She hoisted her sister out the window of the house, and her little body scurried like a rat, looking for cover.

"Hide!" She felt a hand on her shoulders. Before she could vault herself out the window, she was pulled, tripped by her feet onto the ground, slapping it with her back. "Gah!" she grunted; the man jumped atop her. Before she could grab here sword, is hands were clear around her throat, squeezing tighter like vice grips. Gritting her teeth, unable to breathe, she pushed her fingers into the man's throat, but he was too stubborn.

Mirkur pulled the man up, the knife in his hand, thrust it into the chest. The man grunted as he twisted the blade, pulled it out as blood poured from the ground. Another wound, another pierce, and he pulled out again, until the crimson liquid painted the floor, and he fell to the ground. Mirkur took a bloody hand, helped Keneira up from the ground, and another cry, a peasant, one she didn't know pointed at her. "It's her. She's here."

"Get out!" Mirkur cried. "Now!"

He pushed her, tripped her out the window, landed on a bed of hay, flies buzzing. The smell of feces in the air, her heart pounded with screams coming from inside the house. She stood, looked briefly, Mirkur was a bloody mess, barely recognizable, and the several men inside were looking for here, shrieking like one bloody K'hara. The bird of the air of the Abyss, a foul thing. She turned, saw her sister whimpering behind an iron box, and she took her hand, and pulled her up immediately.

"Run, Jera, run!" she squealed.

Keneira, her heart felt like it was going to burst through her chest, and suffer a heart attack before any blade might pierce her, or weapon of bludgeoning her skull open. Her feet took her to the main pathway, and she heard the cries of those calling for her head coming out from behind. She turned her head again, the blood and markings of Mirkur flashed through her, and sweat beaded through her palms, so she squeezed her sister's hand tighter. Her legs lifted up with strides as several people came running at her with violent dogs, and pitch forks.

She turned her gaze forward, and people were pouring out onto the streets as if someone relayed information to her treasonous efforts. Word could get out quickly here, for reasons she knew not, but she kept running. A loud cackle, whistling wind there was, pushing through the cracks between the houses, brushing past her hair, she nearly fell over, and several pieces of scattering debris, fecal matter, hay, bits and pieces of stone from the ground.

"Give us the girl! Give her to us," someone called, hurling a pitchfork at her. She pivoted her feet, the fork thrust right past her head, scratching her face. Hissing, she gritted her teeth, gripping her sister firmly, ignoring her screams of terror.

"You won't take her," she pivoted as the crowd of people drew nearer to her. Bolting away as fast she could, they ran in a straight line forward, getting closer to the road, which of course, she'd have to brave the Abyss, the one place she wouldn't be followed, least not of which, without a torch. "Stay away from my sister!"

A loud crash there was behind her. She turned her head, and the buildings were being struck, creaking with stones as they struck against the flesh of her pursuers. Knew she did, this was not a blessing as buildings came down, the people inside screamed in agony as their own flesh, bones, and blood littered the earth behind her. Only one thing made in this land could collapse buildings. Catapults. Were they that desperate to come after her? Wait. No. This was far worth as smoldering flames scoured over the land, of all things that could be burned. A loud horn, three blasts it made. Three for war. She didn't have time to remember if it was the Nezka, or the Nezkama that the king managed to piss off, but the timing couldn't possibly be any worse!

Horses galloped, clopping their hooves against the stone coming from the right side of her. Hissing, swearing, she was certain had she not gone to the privy before rescuing her sister, she'd have shat her pants ages ago. There simply was too much to pay attention to as she neared the stones leading out of this village, heading further, and further away, towards the Abyss. The soldiers on the horses were clad with armor and lances as they came forward. Snarls and glares to her left side, she saw giant wolves and goats ripping up the terrain with their strides, and the Nezka, that's who he pissed off, rode upon them, flails, and scythes they wielded.

"Keep running!" she cried. As if to assure herself her little sister would run.

Strides came forth with the shaking of the ground. Cries pierced her ears of battle as te hoards came, encroaching upon them. Wolves howling, horses neighing, iron creaking, metal clashing, and shrieks of pains, whines of wolves followed, and the dying screeches of horses followed. Chest pounding, exhaling, sweat dripping from her, she refused to be separated from Jera, who cried. She couldn't tell what it was, the sound of battle around her was too fierce, and far too loud.

"Keneira!" A loud cry, and a horseback. A warrior on a horse with his lance she didn't recognize. Rearing his horse, he charged at her, pointing his weapon at her. She breathed, looking to the ground as the rider hunted her, and a loose cobblestone was what she found. Reaching out, the moving of horses distracted her for but a moment. Lifting up the stone, she hurled it at the horse. The leg of the horse buckled, neighing as the armored rider was flipped off the steed at her feet. Neck cracked, but he was very much alive. She pulled out her sword, stabbed him in the neck, ad sheathed it, running through the seams of battle.

Continuing to run, the soldiers were too distracted with one another, and with what she thought amounted to several turns of the hour glass, she finally made it out of the fray. Turning behind it, a Nezkama came at her, a large creature with a war hammer. Grimacing, she pushed her sister to the side, the beast struck at her. Jumping to the side, the strike hit the ground. Drawing her sword, she struck at the hands, slicing off his fingers. With a deft flick of her wrist, she impaled him in the chest, twisting the blade before ripping it out.

Behind the fallen corpse of the nezkama, she beheld the level of despair already behind her. Men, women, nezkama, lay on the ground with numerous wounds too their body, many trampled underneath thee strides and struggles of the beasts. And both horses and wolves alive littered the ground, and a few pockets of foot soldiers survived, fighting against one another with no hesitancy, and neither side was willing to give an inch.

"Come!"

"I'm scared!" her sister wailed. "And you're, you're hurting me!"

Keneira shook her head and released her grip. "I'm sorry, but we have to go."

"But Keneira!" her sister cried, tears streaming down her face. "My legs."

"The I'll carry you!" Keneira without hesitation put her hands between her sisters armpits, hoisted her up and started walking away from the scene of battle. "But remember, when we get to the abyss, I must light this lantern."

"Very well," her sister embraced her with the hug.

Keneira and Jera arrived at the road, the flames still lit around from the chaos of mis shot catapults. Oil burned, the scent rancid. Crinkling her nose, she looked around her. Surprisingly, there was no sound, save for the now very distant clanking of metal, clashing battle. A siege like this only ended one way, and that of those who lived here, who knew where the food was. The humans of the north would slay the Nezkama and enslave them, they always did, and then, they'd regroup their efforts shortly to find her. If the King was persuasive enough, they'd even dare traverse the Abyss to find them.

"Alright," she said, letting her sister down. She opened the lantern from its top, pulled out some tinder and lit it aflame. "You're on foot now, remember, stay close to me. And if we're ever separated, don't go into the darkness."

"What if there's nowhere else to go?"

A reality that was far too certain for her liking. There was little that could be assured in a time like this, with opportunities running amuck for anyone else looking for whatever it was the King promised them for her head. Clicking her tongue as she looked her sister in the eyes, attempting to give her an assuring smile as her soul searched for the right words to speak. There was nothing significant that came to mind, and while the truth was far from reassuring, she chose to tell her. "Then do whatever seems best to you. But don't wander too far into the dark that you can't find the light again. Always look up, whenever you do, and look for the green orbs in the sky."

"They're gone," her sister pointed.

"For now, yes," she said. "But there are lanterns scattered across the road. And when the morning comes, the green lights will guide you back to safety. Do you trust me?"

"Yes," her sister reluctantly answered. "More than, anyone else."

They walked through the road. The pathway still lit by the preliminary torch set apart to provide the first sanctuary from the Abyss, the cold black fog, of unknown origin. The light from her lantern pushed the darkness away as she approached. The large streams tried to penetrate the light, but to no avail, thank the Four Gods! She hurried with hastened steps, and it was not too long before she and her sister were completely surrounded by the Abyss, the preliminary torch no longer in sight.

Her heart raced settled. Just silence, minus the creaking of her lantern which swayed on one side of her, their steps, silently making their way across the road, and the occasional screech. A familiar one she'd heard before, but fortunately, didn't see what produced it. The K'hara, great birds flew above the Abyss, while at all hours of all days, they were more active when the green lights faded, like they do. With great fear and trembling, that was one horror that would stay away from the light at all costs. They arrived at another milestone, which a stone held an iron rod impaled, and upon it, a lantern. An orb of light, one in which would give them a sense of ease as the arms of the Abyss tried to penetrate this light, and again, to no success. For now, they were safe.

Or so she thought.

Armor clanked in the distance from the direction from which they came. Clopping hooves, and a flame. Jorgon came at her, riding on a horse with a lance. A lantern on the horse's side. A scowl wrote itself upon his face. The horse neighed violently as he pushed the beast towards the light, and the darkness tried to claim him, but the light was too strong, even from that measly lantern. Blood was caked against his face, and a low arm. The horse reared into the light; the lance aimed at her.

Her mentor, her protector. That's the role he was to play, his tradition. She gritted her teeth as if felt like someone stabbed her heart, trying to rip it from her chest. He trained her for years in swordplay, taught her the value of tradition, despite how religiously she tried to escape it, but now, here he was abandoning his tradition. No. That wasn't it. His tradition was, and always will be tied to the House, and through Keneira's actions tonight, the House all but fell. Killing her wasn't betrayal, by killing her, he would be fulfilling his tradition.

"Stay in the light!" she cried, pulling her sister away, releasing her grip. *Don't stray too far.*

Jorgan got closer, so too, the spearhead meant to impale her. Drawing her sword, she swept it up, striking the spearhead. The horse ran past her as the tip of the spear flew up, the metal clanking at the strike. The horse ran in the abyss, and the light protected him. Rearing the horse around, threw the spear at her. She leaned backwards, the spear nearly taking off her head. He drew his sword, charging at her. The horses hooves came, clopping, drowning out her sister's screams. Her sword, she clutched with two hands, aiming for the horse. Nearing her, his blade slashed. She ducked. The blade barely missed her. She cried out, twisting her body as she struck the horse's hind legs with all her strength.

The horse neighed, tumbling down. Jorgan was thrust off the back of the horse, rolling off to the side. The blood on his face was certainly his, as he stared at her, getting up before she could attempt to strike back at him. His gaze, stern as it was, looked at her with rage before turning solemn to his steed. His blade in hand, he walked over to the beast, on its side now, and he impaled its head till it knew no more.

"Give Jera over to me, Keneira, and I might let you live," he spoke. "Stop running."

"No," she said. "You can't have her!"

"Then I'll kill you!"

"You'd not have offered me the chance had you think you can take me," she said. "Least of all," she pointed her sword towards him in the dueling position. "Not in your current condition."

"Had you still the stance ye had yesterday, it matters little," he frowned at her, his sword raised in response. "We're hear because of your actions, Keneira, you are the best student I've ever had."

"You can not do it," Keneira said. "You can live. Just abandon your tradition, and then it's over, and we can leave."

The night was short, and the road long. She wanted it to over, but the more she tarried here, the more and more time people would have to organize and hunt her, should the battles be over. She hoped earnestly, that there was something inside her teacher that would permit him to throw caution in the wind like she had, but actions had consequences. In an ideal world, she never would have asked this of herself, nor asked him to abandon the values he held above everything else. But this world was far from ideal, and no amount of cruelty with the grim pits of despair and ceaseless violence and starvation could or would change that.

"You don't get to decide when it's over," he said. "You don't get to uproot tradition. You don't get to change the will of the King!" sharp was his words before releasing a sigh from his lips. "I gave you an out, just walk through the Abyss, leave your sister to me, and then it will be over. Just leave!"

"You know I can't do that," now she felt herself frowning.

"Then this will be the last fight one of us will know,"

"So be it,"

Keneira clashed with him. Sword against sword, her shoes and his boots in the mud and blood of the horse, spraying, slipping. His strong strikes were significantly weaker than she was used to, caught in the fray of battle, clearly he did with a nasty Nezkama. However, all this to suggest that he was still admirable, pivoting against strikes he normally would have taken. A slash struck towards her, unarmored, she parried it with the pommel, twisting her body, pushing him aside. His free hand twisted into a fist, punching her square in the face. Grunting, she was pushed back on here feet. The dirty trick!

He swung his blade. She bent backwards, the steel nearly nicking her nose, stepping backwards. Dancing, she returned to her feet again, her stance, firm as she could manage. He trust one at her again, and she twisted herself to permit the thrust to past her. She struck his wrist with his pommel, hard. The blade came free. She swiveled the blade to his throat, but he pivoted before she could kill him, a braced moved upwards, parrying the strike. His blade clamored into the Abyss, and he charged at her, tackling her to the ground.

"Keneira!" her sister cried. "Jorgan, stop this, please."

"No!" was his response. "These are the consequences!"

Keneira felt a strike to her face, the back of her head hitting the ground. Grunting, her hand stretched to his waist, pulled out the dagger he kept tucked away in his sheath. Impaling him in his under armor, twisting the blade. He grunted, grimacing, she pushed him off, rolled atop him. Ripped the blade out as blood poured out thee wound. The mentor, she looked him in the eye, a man well respected for his prowess in battle; terror wrote itself upon his face as he was bested, and the knife impaled his neck, his screams silent in the light.

Panting, her mentor was dead, and she leaned back, the blade struck the ground. Blood pooled, ad already, she started to feel it wet her buttocks as she sat in the mess. Her hands shaking, she stared down, and felt a presence behind her. "Keneira," her sister's high-pitched voice brought her to. Her right hand immediately grabbed hold of her sister's arm. *All for you. I doo this all for you.* He teeth gritted once more, and she took the knife, hurled it into the Abyss, screaming. Just a little peace, that's all she wanted now. But there was now only but one choice, standing, ignoring her sister's plea for her to address her, she stood.

"Ha," she grunted, a sharp pain hit through er abdomen. Limping, she reached for her sword, and put it to her waist, and that of Jorgan's, strapped to her other side. "Come, Jera, we must get going. She moved and turned, grabbing hold of the lantern, and looked towards the direction leading South, away from the Kingdom she knew, and she walked towards it. A free hand with her touched her sister's hand, and she was pulled close to her side.

"Very well," Jera spoke, her hair tucked behind her ears. Respectable, she would make someone happy, but not that bastard prince.

"We keep walking, until we're far away from this place, and we can rest," she said. "Then, we'll show you the whole world!"

What kind of promise was that? This world was dark, plant life existed rarely, and that tree, that fruit from yesterday was the most likely thing she'd ever come across in ages. The flowers died, the vegetables died, and those that were deemed unfit for human consumption were tossed to the animals. Breathing heavily, another pain, shooting up, her gaze looked downward. Some dust upon a cobblestone, shaking. Her eyes gaped open in terror, looking upwards, and the Abyss still remained disturbed, save for a few lights, moving along the dark, traversing it with lanterns. Scores of footsteps, marching towards her, from the one direction she was intending on going. Her way had been cut off. Sh could traverse the Abyss, but in the pain she was in, she doubted she could very well outrun a beast, outrun the corruption inside it, and the K'hara especially, still screeching.

What if she was to kill King Crushma? Tradition would come crumbling down with him. There would be no power, and the counts would struggle, fighting one another for the next several years for the King's crown. A fight from the Nezkama soldiers that plagued them now, perhaps it might not be considered the best course of action, and then the humans of the north would end up, unintentionally, enslaved to the Nezkama. But, she was also uncertain, if it was nezkama troop that were in front of her or the king's men. She let out a sigh, there was no good option here. Just the best worst option. But she must still keep her sister close. Or else all her efforts would be rendered meaningless.

"Hey," she said, kneeling down. "We're going to go back."

"Why?" here sister whined. "I don't want to go back to awful men."

"Our way is blocked," she said, pointing to thee Abyss with the faint orange hue of moving flames. "See there? We cannot survive the Abyss for long, so we must go back. I will not let him have you. You hear me, Jera? I will not let anyone have you."

"I understand," she said.

Keneira took her hand and turned. As they passed Jorgan's body, her sister said, "I really liked him."

"I—I know," she stammered. "I did too. There's not much we can do now, just head forward."

The fief was overturned. Flames still scoured, and volunteers were pulling the dead off the streets, dragging them into larger pits, before setting them aflame. Corpses of animals were cut up to pieces for manageable chunks, discarded into wheel barrels, horses and wolves, arms, legs, heads, ribs, thighs, all cut up to pieces, and the blood coated the land. There would be no time to recover, and the fighting all but ceased, and the sound of the marching band behind them, seemed all but insignificant now, but it was still on its way, and in Keneira and Jera's way from escaping, and without resorting to drastic measures.

Her sister whimpered, again, of course, why wouldn't she? Animals, things of the like she loved, and things, of which she took for granted. Life was short and worthless in this world, bleak, despairing. What was the point of any of it? No. She mustn't think like that, not for her sister. She turned to her, knelt down, clasped her hands over hers. "I need you to be quiet," she said. "We're going further in, and we can put an end to them hunting after us. I will kill that bastard King!" here teeth gritted. "And maybe we can save our house, and not have to leave. Unless we do just that, they will never stop hunting us. I need to get closer but—"

"You'll die," her sister said. "Everyone will."

"Not today," she assured her sister. "If I can kill Jorgan, I can kill him. I need you to be close, I can't have you getting too far from me. Stop whimpering, stop grieving, there will be a time for it, just not now. You hear me, Jera?"

"Very well," she said, and put her free hand over her mouth.

"Good girl," she whispered to her.

She led her sister through the village, well, what was left of it. Disappearing behind shattered remains of buildings, stands, people, carcasses, boxes, and various debris. Weapons and shields broken, wrenched into pieces of steel and iron more hazardous to use, than to their intended target. Even the arrows were bent out of shape. Moving further, she heard the distant scream, another battle horn, and the soldiers of the North went back to battle, the Nezkama, now she knew, had prepared another offensive, another wave, but fortunately, most had completely forgotten what she'd look like to be hunting for her in such good measure.

They passed by the fief, and there was a steady line of steel bars, and rope. Looking upwards, creaking, swaying in the wind were several bodies. Blood covered their face, but she recognized them. Her hand turned, holding her sister close so she wouldn't see her father hang there, dead. He was swaying back and forth, creaking, likely croaked, hopefully with the snap, and he didn't have to struggle till te air he breathed was finally snuffed out. And here she was, she and her sister, te last line of their house. There was no two ways about it, this was her doing, and her fault, just to save her sister. Was it worth it? Gritting her teeth, in one fell swoop, her sister had been exposed to the gritty pits that is violence that could only be produced by people.

"Cover your eyes," she said. "I don't want you to see this."

"See what?" she said.

"Trust me," she assured her again. "You do. Not. Want to see this."

She lifted her sister up, and walked her up the path leading towards the temple, but off the beaten path so they wouldn't be seen, the guards and soldiers rushing about to get to the front lines to kill the Nezkama invaders, once and for all. Refreshed as the Nezkama might be, the Northern humans were built of tough stuff. They knew pain, and knew how to suffer, a virtue which the dirty little devils simply knew not. She found a small barn, some hay, and she put her sister atop it.

"Stay here," she said. Her sister need not follow her. It would be needlessly distracting.

"Don't leave!" her sister pleaded, clutching tightly to her forearm. "I don't want to be alone."

"You won't be alone," she pointed at the chickens. "I'll be back. Like I said, Jera, I will not let them have you." She lost too much already. For her. She won't lose her too. "Remember, be quiet, don't let anyone see you until I come get you."

"But what if you don't come back?" her sister pleaded. She'd now seen death enough to know.

"I will come back, I won't die, you'll see. Just stay here," she replied, turning before she could see here sister's eyes glaze over.

The temple was close now, the Four Gods. Reigning supreme with their superfluous ideals imposed upon people who would never know them personally, people who had no business following traditions. The temple, outside it, a bonfire. Mournful music played, still, instruments, her father's musicians, see, they spared them, but not that of the house. Of *her* house. This was the price. She crept up and beheld the king in the center of the circle by the bonfire, mourning, a bed of hay and iron rods, and on it lay his son, on fire, cremating and the ashes of his corpse rising to the Abyss above them.

Gritting her teeth, Keneira's hand rested on the pommel of her sword, and she'd kill the king, right here in front of all these instruments. If her house was to truly die tonight, so too will the kingdom come crumbling down with the man who cursed her existence and forced her father to agree to a child marriage, just to satisfy his sick bastard of a son's debauchery! What else was she supposed to do now? Well, best do this now and get it over with.

"King Crushma!" She darted out from the shadows, charging at the king.

He turned, a grievous face written upon his, and his hand rested on his pommel. Armed to the teeth, and armored heavily with chain mail, and leather patches, he twisted his stance to face her. Eyes red with tears and swollen. The sad face turned ire, grimacing as he pulled his sword up, and he parried it with ease, kicking her a few steps away, and slashed at her. She parried the strike, pushing her further away; she realized the strike he made was merely to put her far away from him, and nothing else.

"Keneira," he spoke solemnly, gritting his teeth as she swung back at him. Pivoting his feet, a swift tilt to his back ensured he'd not get wounded. "You kill a man's son, and as he's grieving seek to take his life. Why would you do this?"

"You know very well why," she gritted her teeth. "And I walked past my husband and father hanging! That only proves my resolve was correct," who was she trying to convince, exactly? "You tried to marry my sister into your family."

"It was your father's choice!" he spoke, and she gasped. Could it be true? "I sent out the word to all the counts, those with eligible daughters for my son, and so too, did he make his choice. Yes, yes, my son has unique disgusting tastes, I know that, but I'd never force a count to decide. They had options."

"I don't believe you," she said.

"Then trust me when I say, your father was the only one willing to submit his daughter to this, to submit your sister!" he said. "Who's the real devil here? My son? The filthy swine? I can't help that. Me, for providing him options? You who killed my son? Or your father who offered Jeanette so willingly? It seems that our fates are more intwined than you might think."

"We're not," she snapped. "We're not. I'll kill you for what you did to my House!"

"What I did?" he scoffed. "You're a literal child!" he pointed a finger at her. "If you had not killed my son, they would still be alive. You'd still be heir to the count's seat. Your treasonous attempt to subvert your father's decision led to that, not me. Your house and mine were tied. Success and failure depended on the other. If the marriage went off, the union would make things more sable, and the line of kings would continue. Now, there is no line to continue, and when I die, we'll be thrust into chaos! Is that what you want?"

"No," she replied. "I just want to kill you."

"Stupid girl!"

Keneira grimaced to charge at him. Their swords clashed, the metal clang. Pivoting forward, her stance remained steady, after all, Jorgan, trained her, but he was not the best teacher in the land, the best was always reserved for the King. She pivoted, tired, as her legs proved to be true, and the King, older in years, was still nimble, dancing back and forth, pulling his blade to try to feint her. They nicked each other's sides multiples times, but with nothing substantial. Grimacing, Keneira knew what might await her should she lose, fail and Jera's life too, was forfeit. Lost her house, lost her husband, her father, and now, her life, and perhaps her sister too. She couldn't lose everything!

He kicked her. She twisted her blade at him when she was pushed back, pivoting, her ankle tripped, and sprained. "Gah!" she cried on the way down. Her hand swept up as the King walked over to her, kicking the sword from her hand, clattering against the ground, it slid, and the King's blade touched her cheek. Crushma, panting, sweat profusely dripping from his forehead. She wanted to push herself up, but his iron boot pushed against her chest, pinning her to the ground.

"Enough of this," he panted. "There is but one way out of this now, where is your sister."

"No," she grunted. "I'll not—" His foot lifted and pushed against her abdomen. The weight forced her to spit ass her body responded to the pain inside her. "Gah! I'll not tell."

"Where is your damn sister!" he said. "I'll not ask again. This is the only way."

"No!" she said.

"Don't you understand, I am trying to save both our houses!" he hissed. "If I adopt her as my own, I can marry her off to someone that will gladly take her. Now, where is your sister!"

"Keneira!" Jera's voice cried.

She turned to where the voice came from. Her sister was there, right in front of Count Mala, whose hands firmly grabbed hold of her sister's shoulders. A sneer was upon her face. How did she find her? Raspy breaths escaped Keneira's lips, still in pain, and her heart thumped hard through her chest. She wanted to vomit. The king looked up, the blade still scratching her cheek with the point, warm blood dripped down.

"Well, I don't really need you now," he said, raising the sword up for an executioner's blow.

"Crushma," Mala opened her mouth. Keneira turned her head from the blade to her sister. Frightened was she, and deservingly so. There was no telling what Mala would do, not with a hostage as now valuable to the King than anything else. Was she trying to help? She was so kind to her last night, if, a little unsettling. "I," she took something out from her side; Keneira couldn't rightly tell what it was. "Had other plans."

Mala took the item, deftly brought it upon her sister's throat, red blood poured down. Coughing, her sister did, and as the blood rolled down the neck into her dress, Keneira cried, "No!" her sister collapsed to the ground. The king swore, as Mala laughed. Her sister, the blood was on her hand. The foot of the King released from her grip, and she sprinted to her sister, crying, tears rolled down her face as she tried to stop the bleeding but alas, the eyes already faded, and the life seeped from her body. Her soul had departed this disgusting world. Jera's life, and her happiness and joy, the innocence behind those eyes was the reason Keneira did anything tonight. Now she was dead.

"You don't get to decide—"

"Keneira killed the Prince, an act of treason, and yet you failed to enact your own justice!" Mala replied. "You're not fit to wear the crown."

"Iit was for the good of the kingdom," he sprinted at her with a drawn blade.

Mala deftly disarmed the King with her dagger, thrusting it in his throat, twisting, his sword clattered to the ground, lifeless, as soon he was. The Count turned to her, and she had nothing to defend herself with. What did it matter. In a single night, her attempt to save her sister from a rotten marriage only got her killed, and so too, the line of the King, and their house was destroyed. Pitted against her mentor, she killed him; her husband, her father, executed, and so too now, her sister slayed right before her eyes.

"Keneira, dear," Mala said. "Why, oh why did you have to go and kill the King?"

Keneira felt a rock strike her in the face.

Keneira groaned. Waking up, she found herself tied, ropes and all, to the bottom of an iron slab. Holes within it, behig tied to four horses. A pain seared through her face, a tongue moved around her mouth. The cheek was swollen from the rock, and the air, had light as she moved, seemed thinner. How long was she out? Where was she? No one around her at all, simply put, she was just where she was. Where was—a vision flashed before her, her sister.

"Jera!" she cried. Seeing her death, a second time wasn't any easier. She lost everything. *I don't want to be alone.* Alone was exactly what she would become.

"You're awake," Mala's voice rang clear through the air. Her dress was beautiful, but for such a person it was ill suited. "Nice to see you again. You ready for another grand adventure? One of which you—"

"Fuck you, you bitch!" She screeched. "Fuck you. I'll fucking kill you!"

"By the Four Gods," Mala gasped. "Here I am doing you a favor."

"After killing my sister, your favor can go throw itself over the wall!" She kicked against the slab to no avail.

"You killed the king," she said. "And plunged the north to chaos."

"You did that you treasonous bitch!"

"Well, you killed the Prince," Keneira gasped. "Since you've been gone, the North quelled the invasion of thee Nezkama. We're whole yet again. We will have a summit as to who will replace him, ad likely get into more petty squabbles. Not that I mind of course," she sneered. "Your house, the King's house, are now combined into one, and whoever is crowned king or queen, I hope yours truly quite personally, will inherit that.
Why, we're practically sisters, now aren't we? Well, you being alive complicates things, for if you were found alive, you'd be crowned, but so many people would ask for your head, you'd barely last a week," she clicked her tongue. "So that you're not surprised, I'm going to tell you what I'm going to do with you.
I'm taking you to the south, selling ye to a brothel. Got a nice fancy reward down there for those who used to own land, which, you very much qualify." She cackled. "You're out of my way, and you get to live. This is a wonderful exchange, if you ask me."

Keneira gritted her teeth, eyes narrowed so she could stare her hatred into Mala's eyes. She hated this count, and soon, perhaps, this queen. She was involved with one royalty assassination, which got botched up so bad it cost her everything. Literally everything, and now, she was to be downgraded to the common whore, used for some miller's breeding sow, no, there would be no breeding into her womb.

Not one bit. She would bite their cocks off before they touched her!

"I will buy my freedom, Mala," she gritted her teeth. "And when I do, I'm going to raise your land to the ground."

"Well, suit yourself, and good luck!" Mala walked past her, all the while cackling at her misfortune.

www.ingramcontent.com/pod-product-compliance
Lightning Source LLC
Chambersburg PA
CBHW031414310726
48971CB00003B/855